Other Books by Douglas Hackle

Clown Tear Junkies

The Hottest Gay Man Ever Killed in a Shark Attack

Is Winona Ryder Still with the Dude from Soul Asylum? and Other Lurid Tales of Terror and Doom!!!

TERROR MANNEQUIN

Copyright © 2019 by Douglas Hackle
Cover artwork by Hauke Vagt
Cover design by Megan Moss

All Rights Reserved. No part of this book may be reproduced or utilized in any form or by any means, electronic or mechanical, including photocopying, recording, or by any information storage and retrieval system, without permission in writing from the publisher. The exception would be the case of brief quotations embodied in critical articles or reviews and pages where permission is specifically granted by the publisher author. This is a work of fiction. Names, characters, businesses, places, events and incidents are either the products of the author's imagination or used in a fictitious manner. Any resemblance to actual persons, living or dead, or actual events is purely coincidental.

Contents

Prologue 1
Chapter 1 16
Chapter 2 31
Chapter 3 35
Chapter 4 40
Chapter 5 45
Chapter 6 48
Chapter 7 54
Chapter 8 62
Chapter 9 67
Chapter 10 70
Chapter 11 73
Chapter 12 82
Chapter 13 85
Chapter 14 92
Chapter 15 97
Chapter 16 101
Chapter 17 107
Chapter 18 112
Chapter 19 118
Chapter 20 128
Chapter 21 131
Chapter 22 139
Chapter 23 142

Chapter 24 147
Chapter 25 152
Chapter 26 155
Chapter 27 159
Chapter 28 177
Epilogue 183

Prologue

Halloween, 1989

A security guard named Roy Malloy awoke with a start, arms flailing and nearly toppling out of his desk chair. Mere moments ago, he'd made the mistake of easing back in his chair, locking his chubby hands behind his fat, mostly bald head, and shutting his tired eyes. *Just gonna rest my eyes for a sec,* he'd thought. And he'd dozed.

Now, sitting bolt upright, the guard glanced over his shoulder to see if anyone had entered the small security office, though he knew the housekeeper and cook had left the house hours ago. He was still alone, thankfully, the door still shut.

Roy turned back to the gloomy monochrome glow of the black-and-white security monitors mounted on the wall above the desk, scanning them for anything out of the ordinary.

Everything looks okay, he thought, breathing a sigh of relief.

Arranged in a rectangular array, the monitors displayed camera feeds of the mostly uninhabited rooms, halls, and immediate exterior grounds of the house. The monitor on the bottom right showed the ground floor: a basement-like, open-floor chamber through which a wide stream of water flowed in and out via arched portals in the room's north-facing and south-facing walls, respectively. Near the center of the room, Roy's employer—eccentric, retired oil tycoon Silas Amadeus Cruthers XVII—sat in a chair along the edge of the stream, his back to the camera, flanked on each side by a tray supporting a large bowl of Halloween candy as he waited for the next group of trick-or-treaters to float into the room on their canoes, kayaks, or inflated rafts. The room itself was a decorated Halloween wonderland: prop ghosts, ghouls, skeletons, zombies, werewolves, devils, and tombstones arranged throughout a floor blanketed in machine-generated fog that lapped at either side of the flowing water, the ceiling dripping with sheets of cotton spiderwebs dotted with plastic spiders, everything washed in the dim light produced by the purple, red, and green light bulbs that burned in the ceiling's recessed fixtures, though the macabre mix of color was only visible as shades of gray on the monitor.

Yep, no harm done, Roy reassured himself. But he really had to be more careful. Falling asleep on the job was a big no-no when you were a security guard. But could anyone blame him for nodding off now and then? CCTV security monitoring in the middle of nowhere at a place like Fallingwater wasn't exactly exciting work. But Roy knew he shouldn't complain. There were far worse things in the world than boredom, and this gig sure beat chasing shoplifters at the mall or escorting belligerent drunks out of overcrowded rock concerts.

By the way, in case you've never heard of it, Fallingwater is a home designed by famed architect extraordinaire Frank Lloyd Wright. Built in 1938 in the woods of rural southwestern Pennsylvania, the house was constructed over a natural waterfall along a steam called Bear Run, itself a tributary of the Youghiogheny River. A celebrated example of modernist and organic architecture, Fallingwater is one of the most famous houses in the world.

Of course I've heard of Fallingwater, you stupid, blithering asshole, you might be thinking right about now.

Oh, yeah? Okay, smart guy/smart girl. But did you also hear that after years of being open to the public, Fallingwater passed back into private ownership when Old Man Cruthers purchased the place from the Western Pennsylvania Conservancy in 1975? Did you hear how the old man subsequently cut off all land access to the house but had the stream deepened and widened for about a quarter mile on each side of the house to make it more navigable by small watercraft, flotation devices, and even swimmers? How instead of tumbling over the fifty-foot waterfall to their deaths, any visitors riding the stream through Fallingwater's ground floor were diverted away from the falls by a submerged grate and redirected down a 400-foot water slide built into the adjacent hillside, a water slide conceived of and paid for by the old man himself? How this slide delivered small watercraft and swimmers alike swiftly and safely down to a deep section of the creek often enjoyed as a natural swimming hole? How for nearly a decade, whenever the weather was fair, people came to Bear Run from far and wide to enjoy what was essentially an extended lazy river ride that ended with a mildly thrilling, family-friendly plummet down said water slide?

And did you ever hear how a Halloween tradition developed in Selohssa—the town nearest to Fallingwater—where trick-or-treaters visited Fallingwater as part of their trick-or-treating itinerary, boarding canoes, kayaks, and inflated rafts upstream from the house in order to make the fun-filled trip? How the old man put up legendary Halloween displays every year for his visitors' enjoyment? How a half-submerged lever-controlled swing gate in the stream temporarily halted traffic in the center of the room, allowing Old Man Cruthers to pass out generous amounts of candy before the gate retracted to let the trick-or-treaters go on their merry way out the other side of the house and down the water slide? How Fallingwater was probably the coolest fucking place in the world to go trick-or-treating??

No, you've never heard of any of that?

WELL, WHO'S STUPID NOW, HUH?

Geez!

Anyhow, Roy turned his attention back to the basement camera feed: Old Man Cruthers reached down to drop candy into three plastic sacks, each already fat with a night's worth of sugary loot reaped by a small Darth Vader, a smaller Teenage Mutant Ninja Turtle, and an even smaller fairy aboard a canoe, the children's father seated at the stern, an oar laid across his knees. In the foreground lurked the army of prop monsters, limbs and claws outstretched, frozen in time in their implied march toward the stream.

Mounted to the exterior wall of the house, another camera showed where the stream split into a manmade fork as it exited the basement, the left side of the fork forming a short, narrow channel that fed into the water slide, the wider channel on the right continuing forward several feet before falling away into the darkness. A steel grate rose about a foot above the water line, crossing the stream diagonally to prevent anything larger than two-inch square from going over the falls.

Yessiree. Everything looks A-okay, Roy thought.

Hm.

Or does it?

He turned back to the ground floor feed, leaned in a little closer to the screen, squinting at the somewhat grainy, low contrast picture, watched the canoe resume its trip down the stream as the old man pulled back the lever to open the swing gate, the children and father waving to him before they floated out the arched exit, the old man waving back at them.

Yet something about the scene was...off. And damned if he could put a finger on what it was.

Roy studied the monitor for a few more seconds before he finally figured it out.

That tall figure standing next to the mummy in the rear of the monster horde—Roy hadn't noticed it before. He used the joystick controller in front of him to pan the camera right and zoom in on it. Except for a pair of pale, spindly legs, the figure was mostly concealed in shadow, its body a top-heavy blob of darkness set against a background only slightly blacker than itself, the direct light from the nearest ceiling bulb not quite reaching the wall by where the figure stood.

Regardless of whatever the thing was, the basement Halloween display had been up for three days now—so why hadn't he noticed the figure before?

The thing executed a wobbly about-face, took two steps forward, slipped out from the shadows into the wan light for the security guard to see it.

Roy now saw that the bulky top-heaviness of the thing was due to it being four figures rather than just one. The larger of the figures was a pale, unclothed, genderless mannequin. Its left arm was bent at the elbow, the forearm crossing its midriff like a waiter with a napkin draped over the arm. Perched on its forearm like a trapeze artist seated on a trapeze was a ventriloquist dummy. The mannequin's right arm appeared to support the dummy's back. On the dummy's lap sat an antique wax doll, its face misshapen and lop-sided. In turn, a faceless voodoo doll sat on the wax doll's lap. For its part, the voodoo doll held onto a plain wooden box that rested in its lap. All four of these connected horrors, even the eyeless voodoo doll, appeared to stare up at Roy though the lens of the security camera.

The image on the monitor dissolved into scrambled, stroboscopic bands of black and white, scrolling vertically and then diagonally across a background of roiling static.

"Wh-what the fuck?"

Roy rose from his chair, grabbed the monitor in both hands, shook it before hitting the side of it with the palm of one hand. A beat later, the scrambled picture returned to normal. Roy scanned the restored camera feed, but the mannequin and its uncanny charge were nowhere in sight. Old Man Cruthers remained seated in his chair, his back still to the camera, presumably oblivious to the presence of any intruders.

Had he just imagined everything? Were the mannequin and its infernal little crew the waking remnants of a dream he'd had during his nap? Only Roy couldn't recall dreaming at all, certainly not about anything like that.

Movement flashed on the exterior monitor.

On the screen, the mannequin emerged outside the house from the exit portal, wading in the two-feet-deep water, the angle of the camera showing an oblique, almost bird's-eye view of the thing and its smaller companions, its steps stiff but purposeful. It stopped before the mostly submerged protective barrier grate. From this angle, Roy saw that the mannequin's right hand did not merely support the seated dummy; the end of the arm was inserted into the dummy's back as if the mannequin were a ventriloquist controlling its mouth and eyes.

The dummy leaned forward, bent its head down to regard the grate, reached toward it with one hand, palm-side up, stubby fingers splayed. It slowly raised its extended arm, causing the metal grate to levitate out of the water as if it had not been securely anchored to the solid rock of the streambed with dozens of long, large-diameter industrial bolts. The dummy's extended arm panned left—as it did so, the grate moved too, in perfect sync with the dummy's motions. In this way, the dummy lowered the grate back into the stream so that it now blocked the passage to the water slide.

Which meant anyone taking the stream through the room would now plummet over the falls.

"Fuck!" Roy yelled, spinning around and knocking his chair over as he scrambled for the door. He grabbed the doorknob, twisted, pulled, but the door wouldn't budge. He yanked harder, shaking the door in its frame, but the thing still wouldn't open. Roy turned back to the security monitors, his panicked eyes finding the screen that showed a view of the main hall on the second floor of the house. Sure enough, someone—or something—had used what looked like a heavy-duty extension cord to tie the security room door knob to the doorknob of the neighboring closet, locking him in.

His eyes darted frantically to the exterior monitor. The mannequin remained standing in the same spot, but now the wax doll had begun to move. That's when Roy saw that the dummy's right arm reached into the back of the wax doll to control it in the same way the mannequin worked the dummy—the wax doll's right arm, in turn, was inserted into the back of the voodoo doll. He now realized he was witnessing the organic movements of a single entity, with the mannequin functioning as the center of will and intelligence, passing its commands down a chain of malevolent ventriloquy.

The wax doll tilted its head back as if to look up at the row of floodlights mounted to the house's exterior wall just beyond the camera's view. Its unevenly spaced eyes—one set much lower than the other—began to glow as it reached out toward the lights with its free hand. One by one, the lights brightened, flickered, and winked out until the camera feed went black save for those two eyes of pinpointed hellfire, the deathtrap now completely hidden to anyone approaching on the stream from inside the house.

Roy turned back to the door, took a few steps back, rammed it with his shoulder a few times, but to no avail. He kicked at the doorknob repeatedly until the thing finally snapped through its bore hole, and the door flew open with a loud crack. He stumbled out into the hall, unbuttoning the holstered S&W revolver on his belt as he rushed down to the stairway. When, huffing and puffing, he reached the bottom of the stairs, he found himself facing yet another locked door. He fumbled with his keys, dropping them once, before he got the right key in the lock. As he did so, muted screams sounded from beyond the door.

But still the door wouldn't open.

He kicked at the knob.

More screams abruptly tapered off in volume as soon as they began.

When he finally broke through, sending a chair that had been wedged under the doorknob flying, he stared straight ahead: Old Man Cruthers and his two bowls of candy were gone. The lever for the swing gate was in the open position. His eyes immediately darted to the exit portal, where he caught the confused and disappointed expression of a young boy dressed as a cowboy who was looking over his shoulder back at Roy from his seat at the rear of a canoe—the boy presumably wondering where on earth Old Man Cruthers was with his candy and why the canoe had not stopped in the middle of the room like it was supposed to—just before the canoe disappeared into the dark of the exit portal.

"Noooo!" Roy yelled as he charged forward.

But it was too late. A beat later, the horrible but brief cries of the canoe's passengers as they plummeted into the darkness assaulted his ears, cut off nearly as soon as they had begun by the unforgiving rocks below.

He dashed to the stream, knocking several prop monsters down into the scattering fog on his way there. Roy knelt down at the edge, where the concrete floor dropped off to form a canal-like channel for the stream. He grabbed onto the lever, threw it the other way, closing the swing gate.

As he did so, he heard a light footfall behind him. Roy sprang to his feet, spun around.

The mannequin, still bearing its three dreadful companions, stood in a pool of macabre green light spilling down from the ceiling about fifteen feet away. Roy now saw each of them in more terrible detail: the mannequin's yawning black mouth like that of an elongated tragedy mask, its oversized eyes, painted wide open as if to betray its own horror at learning some terrible secret, as if the thing were terrified of witnessing its own unholy animation—of beholding its own absurd and improbable existence—terrible eyes that also appeared to silently beg Roy to put the thing out of its misery. Attired in a moldering, colorless suit and bowtie like the deathsuit filched off the disinterred corpse of a long-deceased boy, the dummy was no less unwholesome with its grotesque, cartoonish eyes, its bushy, furrowed eyebrows, and its garishly rouged cheeks painted above a hinged, permanently grimacing rictus lined with large, square teeth like the incisors of a horse. Dressed in a dusty, tattered, vintage gown and bonnet, the wax doll's face was half-melted so that the left half of its rosebud-shaped lips trailed away down to its chin in a dark, runny, tapering smear, its left eye occupying the space a dimple should have held—a pinpoint of fiery orange glowing at the center of each glassy orb. Tufts of Spanish moss poked out through holes in the voodoo doll's crudely-stitched-together skin of coarse burlap. Roy saw a crank jutting out of the side of the wooden box that sat in the voodoo doll's lap. One of the voodoo doll's fingerless limbs rested on the crank's ball-shaped end.

A jack-in-the-box.

The mannequin took a clunky, mechanical step forward. Roy clumsily withdrew his revolver, drawing a shaky bead on the thing's chest. The mannequin took a second step forward.

"Not another step or I'll shoot!"

When the thing ignored his command, Roy unloaded the revolver into its torso. As each bullet slammed home, the thing was driven back a step, its body and the smaller forms of its connected companions juddering with each impact. But the mannequin did not fall.

It shuffled forward, returning to its original position. Though unseen by Roy, the mannequin's right hand manipulated something inside the dummy's body, inducing it to work something inside the wax doll, which, in turn, spurred the wax doll to move its hand inside the voodoo doll. As a result, the voodoo doll commenced turning the crank on the box, whereupon the traditional music-box melody of "Pop! Goes the Weasel" started playing, the tinny, chime-like notes slightly off-pitch.

Still holding his spent, smoking handgun out before him, Roy gawked in slack-jawed horror at the harrowing vision before him, his eyes trained on the box. In those last seconds, as the nursey rhyme melody moved inexorably toward the "Pop!" note, Roy's gut instinct told him to look away or to at least close his eyes, but curiosity got the better of him.

Pop!

The security guard collapsed to his knees, the pistol dropping from his hands and bouncing off the concrete into the stream. He thrust his palms out before him as if to shield himself from whatever it was he saw, his entire body convulsing. In a matter of seconds, twin rivulets of blood sprung from his bulging eyes to leak down his ashen, blood-drained cheeks. The man's heart collapsed in on itself as if crushed by an invisible fist that had reached into his ribcage before transforming into a biologically useless Totino's pizza roll.

Yeah, you read that right.

At the same time, Roy's brain metamorphosed into dogshit—dogshit crawling with plump maggots and fat worms.

Yeah, you read that right, too.

A beat later, the security guard's eyes, now swollen to the size of baseballs, exploded in two pink-red splats. In their wake, the maggoty, wormy dogshit that had been Roy's thinking gray matter only seconds ago extruded slowly out of his ruptured eye sockets. His body pitched forward, his dogshit-oozing face thudding sickly against the damp concrete.

Yeah, yeah, I know Roy's death sounds ridiculous, absurd, and completely made-up, but that's what really happened. In fact, the next morning, after the Fayette County Coroner performed an autopsy on the security guard's body, the cause of death shown on his report read as follows:

> "CAUSE OF DEATH: Heart turned into a motherfucking Totino's pizza roll and brain turned into dogshit. WTF, bitch?!?!!!"

And yes, the usually extremely professional Fayette County Coroner, a respected member of both the local medical and law enforcement communities and summa cum laude graduate of George Washington University's prestigious Department of Forensic Sciences, actually wrote "motherfucking" and "WTF, bitch?!?!!!" in his report!!!

***

In the approximate minute and a half, the gate had been open, Old Man Cruthers along with seventeen people—most of them children—had plummeted over the falls to the rocks fifty feet below. No one survived. In the recorded surveillance video from that night, shortly after the voodoo doll started turning the crank, static inexplicably engulfed the footage, presumably at the exact moment the box's lid popped open.

After the static cleared thirty seconds later, the footage showed the security guard's toppled dead body, but no sign of any intruders. Aside from the grainy surveillance video, the authorities never found any other evidence of the mannequin or its accomplices in or outside the house.

***

In the subsequent settlement of Old Man Cruthers' estate, an unknown beneficiary inherited Fallingwater. As the old man had no surviving relatives and no known friends, people could only guess this person's identity. Later that year, a barbed wire fence, punctuated every fifty feet with signs warning people to keep out, appeared around the perimeter of the 1,500 wooded acres surrounding the house. And where the fence ended on either side of the stream, its three parallel strings of barbed wire continued over the water, strung taut between two end posts lest anyone attempt to enter the property via the water. What's more, a couple dozen signs prohibiting swimming, kayaking, and canoeing sprouted up along the banks of Bear Run at the point where the stream widened just outside Fallingwater's now-conspicuous property line.

Yet despite these security measures, no one appeared to move into the house following the old man's death. A new owner was never spotted entering or leaving the property, either by land or stream, nor was a lighted window ever observed at the place at night.

Over the years, the house went to seed. With workers no longer called in to perform the routine cleaning and preservation maintenance needed to protect the house from the elements, and with no one hired to prune back the surrounding woods, a verdant veil of mildew, moss, creeping ivy, and crawling vines soon overtook the structure's distinctive asymmetrical stone and concrete exterior, making the house less and less visible from all directions. Thus, it came to pass that nature began to reclaim a house that had been designed to conform and harmonize with nature.

Almost immediately following the tragedy, the locals began to tell stories about ghostly figures haunting the woods around the house—the spirits of those unlucky trick-or-treaters who'd fallen to their deaths on that infamous Halloween night. Some people claimed to behold the spirit of Old Man Cruthers himself. And, of course, people told stories about the monster many believed still lurked at Fallingwater and its grounds: a pale mannequin holding a ventriloquist dummy holding an old wax doll holding a voodoo doll holding a wooden box. Some claimed to see this horror either skulking about in the woods or else seated behind one of the high windows of the house looking out, the voodoo doll's stub of a hand always poised on the box's crank, ready to turn it and release whatever horror lay inside back out into the world.

Over the years, the mannequin and its little troupe of connected, nightmarish accomplices came to be known collectively as TERROR MANNEQUIN.

Chapter 1

Thirty Years Later

Forty-year-old Glont Lamont stepped out of a revolving door into the lobby of the Fun 4-Life corporate office building in downtown Selohssa, Pennsylvania, briefcase swinging at his side. Somewhat long and severe in the face and narrow in the shoulders, his dark hair pomaded in a Don Draper side part, the clean-shaven beanpole of a man was attired in a conservative charcoal-gray business suit and looked something like a cross between H.P. Lovecraft, Pee-wee Herman, and George McFly.

And today the dude looked pissed.

"Good morning, Glont," Jill said from her seat behind the gigantic reception desk. In contrast to Glont's good grooming, the young woman was still in her Hello Kitty pajamas and rocking a bad case of fuck hair. As it was two days before Halloween, her desk and the wall behind her were bedecked with paper pumpkins, bats, witches, Frankensteins, and sundry other seasonal decorations.

"Bah!" Glont grumbled. "What's so good about it?"

"Uh-oh!" the receptionist teased. "Sounds like somebody's a big grumpola this morning. Hey, what's with the monkey suit? Did somebody die or something?"

"It's called wearing the proper attire to the workplace, Jill," Glont said as he shuffled past her and headed for the elevators. "Maybe you should try it sometime."

"Yeah, right!"

Glont took the elevator up to the fifth floor in the company of a middle-aged woman in a bathrobe smoking a fat blunt, two old men wearing nothing but black leather thongs and matching studded collars, three cosplayers—one dressed as a Xenomorph alien, one as Nintendo's Mario, and one as Antonio Salieri from *Amadeus*—and a short, bespectacled, mousy, librarian-like woman who, despite refusing to make eye contact with anyone, wore a t-shirt with these words printed on the front:

My great-great-grandparents chomped ass like Pac-Man chomps dots.

My great-grandparents chomped ass like Pac-Man chomps dots.

My grandparents chomped ass like Pac-Man chomps dots.

My parents chomped ass like Pac-Man chomps dots.

Now I chomp ass like Pac-Man chomps dots.

"Wanna puff?" the bathrobed woman asked Glont, proffering him the blunt when the elevator dinged as it reached the fifth floor.

"Bah!" he said with a scowl, clutching his briefcase to his chest as he shoved his way out of the elevator car.

Glont walked the circuitous route to his workstation, which was located somewhere in the middle of the sprawling cubicle maze that was the fifth floor of Fun 4-Life's corporate and operational headquarters. As it was only a quarter past ten in the morning and employees at Fun 4-Life could pretty much come into work whenever the hell they wanted, most of the cubes he passed were still unoccupied. However, some early birds were already "hard at work" at their workstations.

For example, an unshaven twenty-something man naked but for a grubby pair of SpongeBob boxers was kicking back in a leather recliner playing *Grand Theft Auto 5* on Xbox, a lit cigarette dangling from the corner of his mouth, his head cocked and chin held high to keep the smoke from burning his eyes. All Fun 4-Life cubicles were equipped with such recliners, as well as 43-inch flat screen TVs/monitors, high-end gaming PCs, Blu-ray players, all the popular newer and retro gaming consoles, fully stocked bar shelves, refrigerators filled with food and beer, microwaves, and comfy fold-out beds, just to name a few of the standard amenities. A few cubes down from the guy playing *GTA*, a similarly ensconced thirtyish dude watched SportsCenter while sipping from a pitcher of margarita. Just past him, a fiftyish woman was binge-watching some trendy, must-see TV show, while the fortyish dude in the cube across the aisle from her was busy playing some old school Nintendo.

In the time it took him to get to his cube, Glont also passed a few people sleeping off hangovers in their beds, a man taking a break from working on a 3,000-piece jigsaw puzzle to take a pull off an antique Chinese opium pipe, a handful of people swiping idly at their smart phones, and even a few cubes with curtains drawn across their entrances, behind which people were either fapping off to porn videos playing on their big flat screen monitors (judging from all the moaning, grunting, and fleshy slapping sounds), or, if they were lucky, engaging in actual sex. Everyone he passed was either dressed super-casually, ridiculously, scantily, or not at all.

"Hi, Glont," Amanda Baker—the new girl hired not three weeks ago—said to him, her pretty, downturned face slightly blushing. She stood just outside the entrance to her cube, almost as if she were waiting for Glont to walk by, a tall coffee mug grasped in both her hands. (*Psst!*—as the omniscient narrator of this narrative, I'll have you know that she *was* waiting for him to walk by!)

Amanda had the hot nerd chick thing going on: big round glasses, long black hair streaked with purple highlights and braided in tight pigtails, pleated plain jane skirt, green Chuck Taylor low tops, and a tight-fitting *Children of Dune* t-shirt that did little to conceal the two prodigious, ripe, jiggling, grapefruit-like orbs aching to burst out of the tight prison that was the lacy, black Victoria's Secret bra barely containing those bad boys. Like all women in the world, Amanda was more or less constantly aware of her breasts, just as she was also more or less always aware of the way her frilly, silky, Victoria's Secret panties enveloped the supple curvature of her smooth, tanned, unblemished, heart-shaped ass, just as she was pretty much perpetually cognizant of the somewhat pleasantly agonizing sensation of emptiness in her currently unfilled vagina and rectum as they both ached to be filled—a cognizance that was itself just one facet of a more general, distinctly feminine, physical-sexual hyper-self-awareness that also extended to parts deeper inside her body—to, for example, the erotic plumpness of her ovaries, the sexy twists of her fallopian tubes, and the sensual smoothness of her myometrium (whatever the hell that is).

Also, like all other women in the world, Amanda had a small rainbow in her stomach that absorbed all the solid foods she consumed, distributing ingested nutrients to other parts of the body while annihilating all solid and gaseous waste products, which, of course, is why women don't poop or fart. (And should my knowledge of female anatomy and sexual self-awareness and stuff like that not be *perfectly* accurate—man, I dunno—just deal with it, I guess.)

But where was I? Oh, Amanda just said hi to Glont.

Glont paused only to scowl at the woman and utter, "Bah!" before trudging away.

Lastly, he passed his own cubicle neighbor, one Sam Henderson, dressed in full clown gear and busy bouncing on the trampoline that occupied the center of his cube.

"Hey, Glont," Sam said.

"Bah!" Glont said, stopping only to shake his fist at the bouncing clown before ducking into his own cube. Setting his briefcase on his desk, he plopped down into his recliner.

After logging into his computer, Glont pulled up his calendar to see what was on his schedule. He saw that before he clocked out for the day, he was supposed to play video games for at least two hours, watch TV for another two hours, spend at least an hour fucking around on the Internet, and play with his *Star Wars* figures for at least half an hour.

He was also scheduled to get at least mildly drunk and/or high at some point during the day (or all day long, if he so chose), toss off to Internet porn with the ferocity of a madman in an insane asylum at least twice, devour a bowl of spaghetti and meatballs like a pig at a trough (no utensils or hands allowed), and visit the day spa on the first floor for a sauna bath and full body massage. What's more, he was also scheduled to ride (at least twice) the awesome indoor/outdoor rollercoaster that ran through and wrapped around the Fun 4-Life office tower.

Of course, these activities were all merely suggestions: employees at Fun 4-Life could pretty much do whatever the hell they wanted so long as they showed up at the office once or twice a week to log in a least a couple hours of, well, basically anything. If you did at least that, you were guaranteed your base $85,000 annual salary. However, if you followed the company's suggested schedule of daily "work assignments," you earned bonuses that could easily bump that eighty-five grand to well over a hundred grand by the year's end. What's more, Fun 4-Life offered its employees 401(k) plans with 100-percent employer matching, pension plans, health insurance, vision and dental, short- and long-term disability, full tuition reimbursement, and maternity and paternal leave—all of it free. Furthermore, short of tossing your boss out the fucking window, getting fired from Fun 4-Life was nearly impossible.

    Glont turned from the TV screen, clicked open his briefcase: it was stuffed with *Star Wars* figures and nothing else. "Bah!" he grumbled, his face still contorted in a deep, boohoo grimace. He stared down at the figures for a moment before grabbing the briefcase and flipping it up in the air, the figures raining onto the floor around him.

"Whaddya go and do a thing like that for, Glont?" Sam asked. Glont glanced up to his left to catch Sam's painted clown face peering over their shared cubicle wall as the clown reached the apex of his bounce before his head dipped back down out of sight.

"None of your damn business, Sam. And stop spying on me!"

Sam's face rose one more time above the partition, his mouth agape in a mock-offended "o" shape, before disappearing again.

Glont sat on the edge of his recliner, elbows on his desk, hands steepled and resting against his lips, trying to think of something to do.

A-ha! he thought.

After rising from his chair, doffing his suit jacket, and rolling his shirtsleeves up past his elbows, Glont left his cube and took a stroll over to the utility closet, where he grabbed a spray bottle of window cleaner, a sponge, and a squeegee. He then walked over to the north end of his floor and commenced cleaning the windows.

Not twenty minutes later, Marty Strokeoff—the floor manager and Glont's immediate supervisor—approached Glont as he wiped assiduously at a window that did not need wiping. Marty was a middle-aged, heavyset man with a bristly, orange-red neckbeard flecked with gray. As was his habit, Marty was dressed in nothing save a big, safety-pinned cloth diaper and an oversized baby bonnet. He halted a few steps behind Glont, crossed his arms under his sizable, hirsute man boobs. In one hand he clutched a big-ass fucking baby rattle.

"Whaddaya think you're doing, Glont?" he asked.

Glont paused to cast a sharp glance over his shoulder, but immediately turned back to his work. "What does it look like, Marty? I'm washing the damn windows." In front of him, the company rollercoaster zoomed by the window in a rumbling blur.

"We have a cleaning crew to take care of that."

"Yeah, well maybe they missed some spots. A window can never be too clean."

"We need to have a talk, Glont. Follow me, please."

Glont shook his head and spiked the squeegee down on the floor before following his boss down the hall. Marty opened the door to his office, motioning for Glont to enter first. Marty closed the door behind them.

"Have a seat, Glont."

"Aw, man. Do I have to? Can't I just stand?" In Marty's office, "having a seat" meant mounting one end of the seesaw attached to the middle of the floor, and the last thing in the world Glont felt like doing was riding a fucking seesaw.

"I insist," Marty said, gesturing to the seesaw.

"Bah!" Glont sat down on one end of the seesaw, grabbed the handle. Marty mounted the other side, lifting Glont into the air as he did so. The two men commenced taking turns pushing themselves off the floor with their feet.

"Are you unhappy here, Glont?"

"Why do ya ask that?"

"Well, lately you've been showing up to work in a suit and tie when you know doing so is not only unnecessary but discouraged by management. Instead of engaging in fun, recreation, and indolence like the rest of us, you've been making helpful yet unrequested software and hardware updates to everyone's computers, vacuuming the carpets, taking out the garbage, cleaning the toilets, watering the plants, patching the drywall in the men's room, and now you're washing windows. And you're grumpy as hell to boot. And what's with saying 'bah' all the time? Like, who even says 'bah' except for stooped-over old men and characters in Dickens novels?"

Glont sighed. "I'm bored, Marty. I used to love it here. But I've been at Fun 4-Life for fifteen years now. Over the years, I've come to discover that you can only play videos games, watch TV, jerk off, get drunk, get high, eat pizza, and take long naps for so long before it starts to get old, before a desire to do real work gets ahold of you, ya know?"

"No, actually I don't know. Let me remind you that Fun 4-Life in the only company of its kind in the world. For obvious reasons, the turnover rate here is virtually zero, Glont. In fact, a full-time position at Fun 4-Life is probably the most sought-after job in the world, so that whenever we have a new opening, literally *billions* of people apply. Most people would kill to work here. You're one of the very lucky ones, Glont."

"Yeah, yeah, I know all that. But I'm just bored of having fun and chilling out all the time. I mean, I dunno, aren't there any documents around here that need be filed maybe? Some servers to migrate? Some data that needs to be entered in a, er, database? Aren't there like some TPS reports that need to be made? Some machinery that needs operating or fixing? Some fucking coal that needs mining? Some shit that needs shoveling maybe?"

"No, no, no. There's nothing like that to do around here. If you don't mind me asking, how are things at home?"

"Not so bad, I guess."

"You're still living with your nuthouse-bugshit insane mother, right?"

"Yeah. Someone's gotta take care of her and my nephews."

"You mean those two freaks? They're not even your real nephews. Glont, I think your *real* problem is that weird, old house you live in. You're forty years old, man. You should get your own place. You're lonely. You need to make some friends, get a girlfriend. Why, I bet your dick's drier than a dead Mexican armadillo's ass. Maybe you should start thinking about getting married and starting a family of your own, huh? But as long as you continue living at that, that freakhouse, you'll never make a friend in this town or meet a good woman. You do want friends, don't ya, Glont? You want to get yourself a wife one of these days, right?"

"Hey, thanks for your concern, Marty, but my life outside of Fun 4-Life is really none of ;..your business."

"Did Lance invite you to his Halloween party this year?"

Glont didn't respond. Lance Montgomery was Fun 4-Life's director of finance. Glont and Lance had attended grade school and high school together. Lance had always been the most popular guy in school—star quarterback, prom king, most likely to succeed, the whole nine. He and his jock buddies had pantsed Glont in the hallways of Selohssa High and locked him in lockers more times than

Glont cared to remember. Lance had once forced Glont to eat a dried-out white dog turd on the playground in eighth grade. To this day, the dude still liked to brag about how he could barely fit himself into a BigBoy Size XXL condom, the largest condom in the world. In fact, he always made sure to have a BigBoy XXL on his person should the topic ever come up, and he was more than willing to whip out his unwieldy hose, stroke it to hardness, and demonstrate how a fully unrolled, footlong, three-inch wide BigBoy XXL barely contained him.

Lance threw a Halloween party every year at his mansion on the affluent north side of Selohssa—it was one of the biggest parties in town. He always invited everyone at the office.

Everyone except Glont.

Marty interrupted the silence with, "Yeah, that's what I thought."

"Look, I don't give a shit about Lance or his stupid Halloween party! And I care even less about the opinions of a grown man who dresses up like an infant every day. Hey, if you don't like my attitude, Marty, just fire me already...you, you, fat, perverted blob. Otherwise, I'd like to get back to washing the goddamn windows."

Marty bellowed hearty laughter. "You know I can't fire you for something as minor as not doing your job and calling me names. Well, maybe not today, at least. But sometime in the future? Who knows? Maybe the higher-ups will eventually get sick of all your I-wish-I-had-a-real-job nonsense and green-light me canning your ass. I don't really care either way. I did my part by having this little talk with you.

To be perfectly honest, I just wanted someone to play seesaw with. Hee-hee. You can go now."

Without giving Marty any warning, Glont quickly dismounted the seesaw, causing the man to drop hard onto the floor. Glont made for the door.

"Ouch! You asshole!" Marty yelled as he rolled off the plank onto his side, wincing as he rubbed his big diapered butt with both hands. "Fucker! Oh, hey. When you get back to your cube, Glont, tell that bouncing clown it's time for him to change my poopy diaper, will ya?"

"Aw, fuck you, Marty! Go tell him yourself," Glont said as he slammed the door behind him.

***

Glont grew bored with washing windows after a few hours. He was hungry, too, so he went to the cafeteria, got himself a heaping bowl of the gourmet spaghetti and meatballs they were serving that day. Back at his cube, Glont cracked open a tallboy of Coors Light, switched on the webcam that recorded his "work activities," and proceeded to devour his spaghetti and meatballs like a pig at a trough. While he was stuffing his face, an update popped up on his monitor inviting anyone who was interested to save some of their spaghetti and meatballs, knead it into a greasy mush, and then jerk off with the stuff. Doing so was would earn you a bonus of $100.

Eh, why not? Glont thought. He figured he might as well earn some extra cash in between his episodes of workplace rebellion.

When Amanda appeared at his cube entrance to knock on the hard edge of the wall to get his attention, Glont stood before his TV screen, which glowed brightly with a quicksand fetish porn video, his pants bunched around his ankles, his face slathered with marinara, breathing heavily as he thrust himself in and out of a big, greasy glob of mashed spaghetti and meatballs that he struggled to keep from oozing out of his hands. Startled by Amanda's knock, Glont jumped, whirled around to face her, the tasty mush splattering all over the floor. Mortified, he doubled over and covered his nakedness with his sullied hands, but not before Amanda got a good gander of his towering, throbbing, rock-hard, sauce-dripping 4.2 inches.

Amanda immediately pulled an oops face and averted her gaze to the ceiling. "Sorry. I can come back later if it's not a good time." Blushing, she turned to walk away.

"No, wait," Glont said as he quickly pulled up his pants. "It's as good a time as any. What is it, Amanda?"

"I was just wondering if you're going to Lance's Halloween party."

Glont frowned, fixed Amanda with a leery eye. "Did Marty put you up to this?"

"Put me up to what?" Amanda asked innocently enough.

"Ah, never mind. No, I'm not going to Lance's party. He never invites me."

"Would you like to go with me?"

"I told you—I'm not invited."

"But I am. And the invitation said I can bring one guest."

Glont shook his head. "Thanks, Amanda. But even if wanted to go, I couldn't. I have to take my 'phews reverse trick-or-treating tomorrow night."

Amanda arched an eyebrow in bemusement.

"Oh, sorry. I forgot you're new in town. I'm guessing you haven't heard about my 'phews and the whole reverse trick-or-treating thing yet."

"Your...'phews? Reverse trick-or-treating? No, I don't think I have."

"'Phews as in nephews. Reverse trick-or-treating is going door to door on Halloween to give people candy instead of them giving candy to you. Anyway, the whole thing's kind of a long, sad story that I don't really feel like getting into right now. Maybe some other time we could—"

That's when the idea hit him. For many years now, the chore of taking Glont's nephews reverse trick-or-treating had fallen on his shoulders. Back in the day, his mother had sometimes accompanied them, but the osteoarthritis, bubonic plague, and leprosy eventually got so bad that she could barely walk, even with the help of a cane or walker. But last summer, Glont had bought his mom a new mobility scooter for her birthday. He realized he could probably get out of reverse trick-or-treating duty if he had a real, honest-to-goodness date on Halloween. With her new scooter, his mother could totally take them! And surely she would be so ecstatic about his date—it had been many years—that she'd gladly offer to take the boys out for him.

And maybe Marty was right. Maybe it was high time Glont started getting out of his depressing house and began tending to his own emotional, psychological, physical, and social needs instead of always putting the wellness of his fucked-up family before his own.

Plus Amanda was cool. And nice. And hawt.

"Hey, you know what?" he said. "On second thought, sure—I'll go to Lance's party with you."

As a smile played on Amanda's full lips, a sugary-sweet drop of certified organic coconut milk leaked from the exquisite nipple of her mouth-watering left, um, coconut. Not because she was pregnant or because she'd recently given birth (because she hadn't), but because she was very horny for Glont. Because that's what happens sometimes when a woman gets really horny.

Right?

No?

Whatever.

Chapter 2

Construction of its original foundation dating way back to 1640, the Lamont family ancestral home was one of the oldest surviving timber-frame houses in Pennsylvania. The now run-down, sunken, haunted-looking edifice sat at the end of Dapperdog Lane, a narrow, dead end side street tucked away in the working-class south side of town. When Glont arrived home that night, he found his mother, Ruth Lamont—known affectionately as Ma Ruth around the Lamont household—rocking in her rocker and watching TV in the living room in a haze of blue-gray cigarette smoke.

"Hey, Ma. Guess what?"

"I got me a date on Halloween!" his mother squealed. She wrung her bony hands, her tawny dentures framed in a broad thin-lipped smile.

Glont's eyes shot open. "What?"

"I said I got me a date on Halloween."

"But...but that's impossible. You haven't been out on a date in like fifty years. *I'm* the one who has a date on Halloween."

Ma Ruth jerked her head back in surprise. "What? Ya yankin' my chain, boy? Why, you haven't had a date in twenty years. Who in Samhain do ya got a date with?"

"Her name is Amanda. I work with her. We're going to Lance Montgomery's Halloween party."

"Oh, Glont! Aah'm so glad to hear yer talkin' to girls again! But you go ahead and tell that nice girl she'll have to take a rain check, m'kay? 'Cause yer old ma has herself a date that night. Aah'm gonna need ya to take the boys out for reverse trick-or-treat."

"Now wait a minute. How come your date is more important than mine? I mean, you do want to have grandkids one of these days, right, Ma?"

"Sorry, son. But my fifty-year dry spell trumps yer twenty-year dry spell. Why, I haven't been out with a feller since your father ran out on us when he left me for that quicksand porn actress he got smitten with—that quicksand-sinkin' little slut!—so this is very important to me. Old Crub and I are gonna have ourselves a grand ol' time."

"Old Crub! Please don't tell me you're going out with Old Crub."

"I most certainly am. Old Crub's as fine a gentleman bachelor as any in this town."

"Gentleman? That guy's the town drunk *and* the village idiot, Ma! He lives in the friggin' sewers! He's filthy, homeless, diseased, and nuthouse-bugshit insane. Not only that, but he served fifty years in prison for butchering his wife and five kids with an axe and cannibalizing their bodies. And he's a goddamn ghoul and necrophiliac to boot! Old Crub's been caught having sex with dead bodies in the cemetery and eating them on dozens of occasions. Not only that, but he's a racist, Ma! Old Crub's a registered Nazi and former treasurer for the KKK. Shit, the dude still dresses in blackface most days!"

"No one's perfect, Glont. Judge not, lest ye be judged, boy! And it's not like there's hordes of male suiters linin' up outside our front door these days to see me, is there? Plus, I've always wanted to make love to a black man."

Glont made a loud, smacking facepalm. "Ma, you do know that blackface is not the same thing as being black, right?"

"Aw, don't split hairs on me, son. It's close enough! I'll take what I can git. It's not so easy gettin' dates when yer nearly ninety years old and the only gal in town sufferin' from both bubonic plague *and* leprosy."

Glont shook his head in dismay. "Well, what the hell is Old Crub gonna do—pick you up on his damn skateboard? That guy doesn't have a car."

"Aah'm gonna pick 'im up on my scooter. Gonna need ya to hitch Tom Two's wagon to the back so Old Crub has a place to sit."

Glont shook his head in vexation. "Ma, I'm sick of taking Tom Two and The Membrane reverse trick-or-treating every year."

"Hey, you watch yer mouth!" Ma Ruth said in a stern but lowered voice as she turned to eye the open doorway that communicated with the main hall, beyond which was a staircase leading up to the second floor. "They might hear you."

"Can't someone else take them reverse trick-or-treating for once?"

"And who, other than you and me, is gonna take 'em, huh?"

Glont sighed. His mother was right. He knew there was no one else. The rest of the town hated Tom Two and The Membrane. In fact, the town's communal hatred of them was precisely the reason why Tom Two and The Membrane *had* to go reverse trick-or-treating every Halloween.

The rapid thumping of light footsteps descended the creaky staircase, as of those made by a small child, prompting Glont to turn toward their source. And who should appear in the doorway a beat later?

Why it was none other than Tom Two himself!

Chapter 3

You know the iconic screaming figure in Edvard Munch's painting *The Scream*? Well, imagine if that figure fathered a tiny little son—a sort of Mini-Me (or Mini-Scream, as it were)—and you basically had Tom Two. Standing only three feet tall, Tom Two had the same sort of hairless, oversized, upside-down, pear-shaped head as the famous screamer, the same elongated, askew, horror-stricken face, and the same lipless oval of an aghast mouth. He even wore a sooty, robe-like garment that was quite similar to the one depicted in the painting, if not an exact copy.

In fact, but for the sombrero that sat perpetually on his head—the hat was bigger than him, the back of its broad brim always dragging on the floor behind him like the train of a wedding gown—Tom Two was the spitting image of Munch's screaming figure, albeit in miniature and just a tad bit chubbier.

As far as anyone knew, Tom Two had always lived in the 350-year-old Lamont ancestral home, though no one knew where he came from originally. Yet each successive generation of Lamonts had always taken care of him as if he were one of their own, though they were careful to keep him from leaving the property lest he terrify the children of the neighborhood, Halloween night being the exception.

Nearly forty years ago, Glont's grandmother took Tom Two to visit the family doctor for a checkup, seeing as how nobody knew when the little fellow had last—if ever—seen a doctor. In the examination room, the understandably apprehensive doctor called in a few of his colleagues to join him. Owing to this strange little being's odd physiognomy and their inability to determine his age, the docs took a great interest in Tom Two. Regarding their many questions, Tom Two himself was little help as he was mute as a maggot. And while he certainly could have communicated with the doctors via sign language and even rudimentary writing and drawing, Tom Two played dumb with them. He answered most of their questions with a befuddled shoulder shrug.

Ultimately, the docs' interest in Tom Two led to a carload of suited CIA agents visiting the Lamont house a few weeks later, at which time they grabbed the little fellow and spirited him away to a hidden government research facility. After running an untold number of tests on Tom Two, including an advanced radiocarbon dating test that worked on living things, the astonished researchers determined that, in absolute defiance to all known laws of physics, not only was Tom Two *exactly* two years old, but he was *constantly* two years old—i.e., all the cells in his body refused to age one millisecond beyond two years.

So while Tom Two's physiological age was always exactly two years old, no one had any way of knowing how old he "really" was—i.e., how old he was in the timeline of the rest of the universe. As such, he could have been born or created eons ago for all anyone knew. And barring any sort of fatal injury, the whole perpetually-two-years-old thing basically made him immortal.

Though the white coats studied Tom Two for years, his little body refused to reveal any of its secrets: all attempts to understand the time-defying mechanics of his strange cells and all efforts to duplicate those mechanics in the laboratory failed miserably. And again, even if Tom Two had had something of interest to tell his inquisitors, he played dumb for the entirety of his confinement.

So, after five years of Tom Two getting poked and prodded in that research facility-cum-prison, a government car finally pulled up to the Lamont residence one afternoon to drop the poor little bastard off. Turned out that despite Tom Two's singularly extraordinary nature, there was simply nothing the scientists could learn from him.

The conclusion of the government's final peer-reviewed report on Tom Two—a report made public—read thusly:

> *"Conclusion: We must therefore assume that Tom Two is some sort of fucking weird-ass, witchcraft- or voodoo-spawned ABOMINATION OF NATURE! WTF!!!!! Now get his creepy little ass outta here already!!! And while you're up, go pour me a stiff drink!"*

***

After he appeared in the doorway, Tom Two raced over to Glont, latched onto his leg. The little dude was shaking.

"Double T!" Glont said, looking down at Tom Two and laying a hand on his sombrero-crowned head. "What's wrong, my man?"

"They was watchin' skeery movies again upstairs," Ma Ruth said.

Glont stooped down, grasped Tom Two under his arms, lifted him up like a baby. Cradled in the arms of his uncle, Tom Two's shivers began to subside.

"What scary movies did you guys watch, Tom Two?" Glont asked.

Tom Two's stubby arms, little hands, and nubby fingers gesticulated rapidly as he responded in sign language.

"You guys watched *Taken 26*?" Glont asked, his voice edged with admonishment.

Though Liam Neeson had passed away years ago—in fact, only days after the U.S. release of *Taken 12*—*Taken* movies had continued to be released ever since. However, beginning with *Taken 13*, every subsequent *Taken* film consisted of 90 minutes of continuous, unchanging, murky green video footage recorded by a night vision camera installed inside Liam Neeson's actual coffin, so that the posthumous-Liam Neeson era of the *Taken* franchise was essentially a chronicle of the actor's real-life decay in his actual grave. By the time you got to *Taken 24*, you were basically just staring at a skeleton for an hour and half.

"I told you not to watch those *Taken* movies," Glont scolded him. "At least not anything after *Taken 12*. You're gonna have nightmares tonight."

"And they was watchin' dirty movies, too!" Ma Ruth tattled.

Glont smirked. "How did they get access to dirty movies?"

"The rascals ordered Hustler TV!"

Glont lowered Tom Two to the floor. The diminutive figure took a couple steps backward, craned his neck back to regard his uncle. Again, he gesticulated animatedly: *It was The Membrane's idea. I tried to stop him.*

"Oh, I bet you tried to stop him," Glont said.

Tom Two's elongated wraithlike face blushed as he continued to sign at him.

"You guys watched *She Chomps Dad-Ass Like Pac-Man Chomps Dots - Part 8?*" Glont said, wide-eyed. "C'mon, Double T. You know you're not allowed to watch those kind of movies. Christ, you're only two years old."

Just then, a slithering, slinking, skulking, sneaking, snaking sound—something like a wet towel dragging itself down the staircase—reached Glont's ears, prompting him to turn toward the doorway. And what should appear there a beat later?

Why it was none other than The Membrane itself!

Chapter 4

The Membrane was, well, a membrane. And if you think Tom Two was creepy with the whole simultaneously-ancient-while-being-perpetually-two-years-old thing and the whole looking-like-the-screamer-from-the-Munch-painting thing, well, The Membrane—or *'Brane*, as Glont sometimes called him—was fifty times creepier.

While Tom Two was always vague and inconsistent about any memories of his potentially ancient past, he remembered when he first met The Membrane with great clarity. Although he couldn't put an exact date on the occasion, Tom Two had discovered the slimy thing back when the Lamont house was still new, back when the house sat on a dirt road miles away from any other human settlement, surrounded by hundreds of acres of farm fields.

It first appeared in the corner of the cellar, initially as a greasy, silver dollar-sized spot on the field-stone wall, twitching every ten minutes or so as if of its own volition. Over a period of weeks, Tom Two watched the strange organism slowly secrete from the wall, expanding from that small blotch into an ellipse roughly four feet high before peeling itself from the wall and dropping to the floor. At that point, Tom Two went to Ezekiel and Martha Lamont—Glont's great-great-great-great grandparents—and told them about the strange thing he'd found in the cellar.

Understandably, these pioneering God-fearin' Christian folk were repulsed by the creature and wanted to remove the thing from their house. But Tom Two wanted to keep it—he wanted the damned thing to be his little brother. After he threw a shit fit, the Lamonts reluctantly agreed. Tom Two named the thing The Membrane.

For a biological entity that was essentially a pale, translucent sheet of skin-like tissue marbled through with spidery blue veins and often glazed in a clear, watery mucus, The Membrane got around pretty well by pulling, pushing, creeping, crawling, and dragging itself around like some sort of deflated blob. Despite lacking any obvious sense organs, The Membrane could see, hear, and smell as well as most people. Highly intelligent to boot, it was able to do things like add sums, subtract differences, read books, play chess, and order Hustler TV.

Remember how a carload of government agents took Tom Two away to study him for five years? Well, those same agents also got word of the existence of Tom Two's even weirder "brother," which they abducted shortly after apprehending Tom Two. As in the case of Tom Two, years of testing and intensive research left the scientists with no clue as to what the fuck The Membrane was, though they observed that The Membrane's cells were not perpetually two years old like those of Tom Two. But how the bizarre organism displayed a high degree of intelligence, had a functioning circulatory system, and possessed complex motor skills without the benefits of having a brain, heart, or muscular skeletal system remained a baffling mystery.

So, as in the case of its brother, after years of The Membrane getting poked and prodded by the white coats, a government car eventually pulled up to the Lamont residence one morning and dropped the thing off.

The conclusion of the government's final peer-reviewed, publicized report on The Membrane read as follows:

> *"Conclusion: Therefore, we can only assume that The Membrane is some sort of fucking weird-ass, unholy, witchcraft- or voodoo-spawned ABOMINATION OF NATURE like its brother, Tom Two! WTF!!!!! Now get this thing the hell out of here already!!! And while you're up, go pour me a stiff drink!"*

***

"Just the membrane I wanted to see," Glont said as The Membrane crawled into the living room. "Is it true that you ordered Hustler TV today and watched *She Chomps Dad-Ass Like Pac-Man Chomps Dots - Part 8*?"

The Membrane slid next to Tom Two, reshaping itself so that two arm-like appendages rose from its bulk. The limbs themselves grew hands, which sprouted plump fingers that waved about in the air, gesticulating in proficient sign language.

"Oh, so it was Tom Two's idea, huh?" Glont asked, interpreting. "Tom Two forced you to watch it? Yeah, right. Hey, listen. Ma Ruth and I don't really care what *you* watch on TV. You're legit hundreds of years old or something. But Tom Two's only two. So the next time you want to watch porn, do it in private."

Tom Two signed at him to object: *I might be eons old.*

"Well, whether you like it or not," Glont said, "you're *also* two years old. But never mind that. Now, listen. Halloween is in two days, and I was just thinking that since you're such a big boy now, Tom Two—and possibly even eons old, as you just pointed out—maybe you and 'Brane can go reverse trick-or-treating without adult supervision this year, eh? Just the two of you. All by yourselves. Whaddaya guys think?"

Tom Two immediately shook his head before signing: *You have to take us reverse trick-or-treating 'cause I'm only two.*

"Hey, what happened to being eons old?" Glont said. "C'mon, man. At least be consistent."

Tom Two rushed forward, latched onto Glont's leg again.

"Aw, look, he's a-skeered!" Ma Ruth said. "Put yerself in his shoes. Would ya wanna go reverse trick-or-treatin' without an adult, what with all dem mean people starin' atcha and sayin' awful things to ya all night long?"

"It's perfectly safe, Ma," Glont said.

"Even if it is, that doesn't mean it's not skeery for him."

"But he'll have The Membrane to protect him."

That's when The Membrane sprang forward and latched onto Glont's other leg, trembling in fear worse than Tom Two.

Glont sighed heavily, rolled his eyes and stuck out his tongue in protest of the situation. "Alright, alright," he said grudgingly, patting the crown of Tom Two's sombrero with one hand and the slimy back of The Membrane with the other. "Guess I'm taking you guys reverse trick-or-treating again this year."

He cast a gimlet eye at his mother. "But the way things are going, Ma Ruth is never going to get any friggin' grandkids."

Chapter 5

After Tom Two and The Membrane let go of his legs, Tom Two signed up at Glont: *I want to go regular trick-or-treating this year.*

"Sorry, big man," Glont said as he crouched down to Tom Two's level, "but that's impossible."

Tom Two continued to sign at him. It was the same scene every Halloween: Tom Two would object to not being allowed to go regular trick-or-treating like all the other kids, and Glont would have to remind him of the great importance of reverse trick-or-treating.

The tradition of reverse trick-or-treating went back hundreds of years, back further than anyone in town could remember. In fact, Selohssa's collective memory of the time Tom Two had resided in their town was inseparable from the tradition of reverse trick-or-treating itself. For the townspeople had always feared and hated Tom Two, whom they regarded as a monster. Later on, they felt the same way when they learned of the existence of The Membrane. And although the two weird beings did not pose any sort of threat to the town like, say, a homicidal monster such as TERROR MANNEQUIN, the townspeople despised Tom Two and The Membrane just as much as they feared the fabled, diabolical boogeyman that purportedly lurked around Fallingwater.

The only way the townspeople permitted Tom Two and The Membrane to live in their midst—even confined to the Lamont house 364 days a year as they were—was if the pair set out on Halloween night every year with overfilled sacks of candy to pass out to all the town's inhabitants in a practice that was as much a form of ritualistic tribute as it was a cruel walk of shame.

Should the pair ever fail to bring candy to even one inhabited house in Selohssa on Halloween night, then the people had permission to kill Tom Two and The Membrane, or at least drive them out of town.

"Yeah, yeah, I know you want people to put candy in your bag instead," Glont said. "And I know you want to dress up in a Halloween costume like all the other kids, but that's against the rules. We'll have our own little Halloween party back here after you guys finish—just like we always do—with lots of candy and treats. And you can dress up as whatever you want. We'll watch a scary movie, too. How's that sound, Double T?"

Tom Two's ghostly, oblong face wore a crestfallen expression. He did not reply.

"C'mon, my dude. Cheer up. Hey, what scary movie do you want to watch on Halloween?"

Taken 27, Tom Two signed in reply.

"Sure, we can watch that," Glont said. "And what do you want to dress up as for our Halloween party?"

Tom Two signed, *Liam Neeson as seen in Taken 27.*

"Well, that's should be pretty easy. All we have to do is get you a black suit and a skull mask. How about you, The Membrane? What do you want to be for Halloween?"

The Membrane flailed its appendages in response: *A goddamn, motherfuckin', pussy- demolishin' hustla!*

"Eh, I don't think so, 'Brane. How about Harry Potter? Or Iron Man? Or a ghost or a pirate or something?"

How about you go choke to death on a big, blue, molasses-sweet, spiked dick? was the Membrane's signed response.

"Why you!" But before Glont could reprimand the thing further, The Membrane pulled from one of its loose membranous folds a pie container filled with rotting animal guts. The creature then shoved the "roadkill pie" (one of The Membrane's favorite pranks) into Glont's face.

Glont wiped away the jellied blood, sticky squirrel and raccoon intestines, and wriggling maggots from his mug, flinging the offal onto the floor. As he did so, the Membrane scuttled out of the living room, into the hall, and up the stairs, inciting laughter from both Tom Two and Ma Ruth. Though soundless, Tom Two's mute laughter was gut-busting nevertheless. For her part, Ma Ruth convulsed with the labored, dry, croaking cackle of a veteran heavy smoker, her hacking guffaws accompanied by a steady, unchecked trickle of brown sputum flecked with cherry-red, oozing freely down her pointy chin to pool in her lap.

Glont shook his head. "Man, who the heck needs enemies?"

Chapter 6

After Glont cleaned himself up, he prepared dinner for the family. The only thing Tom Two ever ate for breakfast, lunch, and dinner was SpaghettiOs with meatballs. The Membrane was the same way, but with Totino's Party Pizzas. This was a good thing, as money was tight; the Lamont home was heavily mortgaged and taxed, and Ma Ruth's leprosy and bubonic plague medicines were outrageously expensive.

Tom Two was a SpaghettiO-eating machine, his spoon dipping into his bowl just as rapidly as it ascended to shovel the o-shaped pasta into his oval-shaped mouth in a continuous loop until the bowl was empty. The little dude could finish off a family-sized can by himself in under a minute. For its part, The Membrane completely enveloped its Totino's Party Pizzas, liquefying them with a secreted digestive acid and completely absorbing the resultant goo. It was pretty grody to watch. That evening, Glont got the usual for his nephews and reheated some leftover Chinese takeout for Ma Ruth and himself.

"Phone ring much today?" Glont asked as he chowed down on his chicken chow mein at the kitchen table.

"'bout a dozen pranksters," Ma Ruth said.

It was that time of year again: the time when some of Selohssa's more impatient residents called the Lamont household to harass Tom Two and The Membrane in overeager anticipation of the yearly reverse trick-or-treating spectacle. For that reason, Ma Ruth and Glont didn't answer the phone much at all during the month of October.

"Well, why were you answering the phone?"

"In case Old Crub called for me, stupid."

Glont rolled his eyes.

After the boys helped Glont clear the table and wash the dishes, everyone migrated to the living room. Ma Ruth settled back into her rocker and said, "How's about a song from Tom Two?" As she spoke, Tom Two's weird, wobbly eyes widened in excitement, and he shuffled off to the hallway closet to fetch his tuba.

Seated on the sofa, Glont faked a yawn and a stretch. "Ya know what? I'm getting pretty tired. Think I'm gonna go up to bed now. Had a long day at work, ya know."

"Long day at work, my bony old butt!" Ma Ruth said. "What do *you* know about long days at work? What, did ya have a long day playin' yer video games, drinkin' beer, smokin' dope, stranglin' yer little snake, and bein' lazy and takin' naps? Now, you stay down here and listen to Tom Two play a song for us!"

Glont groaned.

Tom Two dragged his tuba to the center of the room. Dwarfed by the thing and standing behind it, he positioned the instrument so its bottom bend rested on the thinly carpeted floor, the bell pointing up at the ceiling.

"What are ya gonna for play fer us, sweetie?" Ma Ruth said.

Tom Two's arms and hands wagged in response: *"Mary Had a Little Lamb."*

"Let's hear it!"

Before Tom Two pressed his lipless mouth to the mouthpiece to blow the first note, Glont clamped his hands over his ears. The Membrane, who had spread itself out on the floor not far from Glont's feet like some throw rug from hell, did the equivalent by crumbling itself into a ball. They both knew what was coming.

The slow, lumbering succession of booming, fart-like tones Tom played was intended to be "Mary Had a Little Lamb," but was more like a very rough rhythmic approximation of the song, each harsh note blown wincingly out of key. After mangling the simple melody a few times, he launched into an improvised solo, pumping those valves as fast as his little fingers would go, producing something that sounded like an elephant causing a multi-car pileup on a freeway.

The only one present who enjoyed the music was Ma Ruth, but only because she was nuthouse-bugshit insane. She rocked back and forth, cackling and clapping her splayed hands in a furor, mouth agape, tongue wagging around like a big pink maggot as a mixture of sputum, blood, bile, diarrhea, and Bulgarian clown jizz bubbled out of her mouth.

(Not sure where the Bulgarian clown jizz came from—well, from a Bulgarian clown, obviously, or else it wouldn't be "Bulgarian clown jizz," but that's about all I know about that.)

The corded phone mounted on the wall in the kitchen rang: *BRRRINNNNNNNNNNNNNNNNNNN-NNNGGGGGGGGGG!*

Tom Two stopped playing as Glont withdrew his hands from his ears. "I'll get it," he said a little too enthusiastically as he rose from the sofa. Anything to get away from that tuba.

"Oh, I bet it's just another prank caller," Ma Ruth said.

"It could be Old Crub callin' for ya, Ma." Glont went into the kitchen, grabbed the phone from its base. "Yellllow," he said into the mouthpiece.

"Is Tom Two there?" an older adult male voice said.

"Yes, he is. But he's not taking any calls right now. Can I take a message? Who may I ask is calling?" Glont's tone was overly cheerful.

"Is The Membrane there?"

"Yes. But The Membrane's not taking any calls either. Mr. Peterson, is that you?"

There was a short pause on the other end. "Yep, it's Bill Peterson." Mr. Peterson owned the barbershop in the square downtown. The only barber in town, the old man had cut Glont's hair ever since Glont was a boy.

"Yeah, if you'd leave 'em a message from me, I'd sure appreciate it, son," he said, before clearing his throat. "Tell Tom Two and The Membrane that I said FUCK YOU!"

Glont heard people laughing in the background.

"And tell those two freaks I HATE 'EM! And tell 'em I said THEY SHOULD JUST FUCKIN' KILL THEMSELVES ALREADY! Heh-heh-heh."

"Well, fuck you too, Mr. Peterson, ya old-ass, Wilford Brimley-lookin' motherfucker."

Glont slammed the phone back on the base. He grabbed a can of beer from the fridge, cracked it open, and went back into the living room.

"I told ya," Ma Ruth said.

"Well, I think I'm gonna head on up now," Glont said, prompting Tom Two to sign at him.

But I'm not done with my song.

"Jesus Christ," Glont mumbled under his breath. "Alright, but make it quick."

Glont plopped back down on the sofa, set his beer on the coffee table, and pressed his hands back over his ears while The Membrane bunched itself into a ball again on the floor.

Tom Two resumed playing with even more gusto than before, producing a cacophony of near-suicide-inducing noise. He kept playing and playing and playing—in fact, his little rendition of "Mary Had a Little Lamb" went on for three and a half hours before he finally set his tuba down and took a couple polite bows.

Though sorely tempted, Glont didn't have the heart to try to sneak away during the performance like The Membrane did one hour into it. Ma Ruth passed out in her rocker just minutes after Tom Two resumed playing. About two hours in, despite Glont protesting that he could hear the tuba just fine, Tom Two insisted on dragging the instrument next to couch and positioning its bell just inches away from his uncle's face so that he could hear it better.

Glont felt sorry for Tom Two—sorry that he looked like the screaming figure from *The Scream*, that he was basically trapped in their house, that everyone in the world other than Glont, Ma Ruth, and The Membrane hated him. Also, even if he was eons old, the dude was only two—a physically deformed and temporally defective child neither understood nor accepted by the cruel world in which he lived.

The least Glont could do, he figured as he sat with his hands clamped over his ears and his head practically inside the instrument's big brass mouth, was sit through this maddening music.

And if Tom Two's tuba did end up driving him nuthouse-bugshit insane one day, then so be it.

Chapter 7

Glont dropped into the office late in the afternoon the next day, went straightaway to Amanda's cube to let her know he would be unable to attend Lance's party with her. When he arrived at the entrance to her cube, the words "Hey, Amanda," ready on lips, he raised one fist to rap his knuckles on the top of the cube wall, but halted abruptly. There in Amanda's chair sat Lance Montgomery. Amanda stood behind him, massaging the man's broad shoulders. She glanced up at Glont, her eyes bulging with a caught-red-handed look before she sighed, her face going sad.

"Oooo, yeah that's the spot," Lance said, smiling, his eyes shut. Just as Glont did an about-face, intending to go right back the way he'd come, Lance opened his eyes.

"Glont Lamont!" he barked. "Stop right there. Where do you think you're going, fuckface?"

"Oh, just back to my cube, is all."

"But it looks like you stopped here for a reason. Do you want to talk to Amanda?"

"Um, well, yeah. I guess so."

"Well, don't mind me, egghead. Go ahead. Talk away."

Glont dry-gulped before he continued, now with a stutter. "Um-um-Amanda, I'm sorry, but I just wuh-wuh-wanted to tell you that I can't go wuh-wuh-with you to the party tuh-tuh-tomorrow. I have to take my nuh-nuh-nephews reverse trick-or-treating. Maybe some other night we could—"

"Okay, that's enough, retard," Lance said, thrusting out a big open palm to shush him. "Hey, don't feel too bad about having to cancel. She wasn't going to go with you to the party anyway. She'll be coming by herself." He turned in his chair to run his wolfish gaze up and down Amanda's body, licking his lips. "See, I just recently became aware of Miss Baker and her, um, *ass*ets. Just this morning, in fact. And I promoted her. Starting tomorrow, Amanda will be joining my team of smokin' hot administrative assistants up on the fifteenth floor. Well, don't be rude now, Lamont. Congratulate Amanda on her promotion."

"Congratulations on yuh-yuh-your promotion, um-um-Amanda."

"*Um—um—um—Amanda!*" Lance mocked him. "Hahaha!" He rose from the recliner, pointed a large, bratwurst-like finger at Glont. "Hey, rumor has it you think your dick's bigger than mine."

"Um, no. I don't think that, Lance."

"It's Mr. Montgomery to you, shithead! Or sir!"

"Suh-suh-sorry, Mr. Montgomery."

Ignoring Glont's denial of his accusation, Lance reached into the front pocket of his chinos, pulled out an unopened BigBoy XXL. "Did you know that I can barely fit into one of these fuckers? Hey, if *your* dick's so great—ya braggart—then let's see how *you* fill one out." He tossed the condom at Glont like a ninja throwing star. It glanced off his forehead, dropped to the floor. "Let's settle this right here and now, Lamont. Let's see who fills out a BigBoy XXL better, huh?"

"Um, no thanks, suh-suh-sir. I'm sure you'd win."

"You're goddamn right I would!" Lance said, brows knitted, the veins in his temples bulging with unfounded anger. "Now here's what I want you to do, moron. I want you to take that condom out of its wrapper, pull the damn thing over your stupid head—pull it all the way down to just above your mouth so you can still breath. Because this, my friend, is the only way *you'll* ever fill out a BigBoy XXL. Heh!" Grinning, he turned to Amanda to see if she was as impressed as he was at his clever joke.

She lowered her gaze to the floor, unamused.

"Yes, sir," Glont said. He did as he was told, though with some difficulty. Eventually, he got the condom to envelope more than half his head, the tight, translucent mask distorting his face and turning up his nose to make him look like a pig.

"Perfect. Now get down on the floor on your belly and army crawl all the way back to your cubicle."

For just a second, Glont was tempted to tell Lance to go fuck himself, to quit Fun 4-Life right there on the spot. But despite all his rebellious talk and attitude, Glont knew his family depended on his salary to pay their five mortgages, the outrageous utility bills, and the exorbitant inheritance tax on their ancestral home, not to mention the cost of Ma Ruth's bubonic plague and leprosy medicines, which had been unscrupulously priced ever since Martin "Pharma Bro" Shkreli had acquired their patents the day after he'd gotten out of prison. But on the plus side, Glont realized the combined act of pulling the condom over his head and shame-crawling back to his cube was probably the closest thing to real work he had ever been asked to do at Fun 4-Life.

So, despite his old, deep-seated hatred for Lance Montgomery, his present humiliation, and the sting of disappointment he felt at losing any chance he might have had with Amanda, Glont said, "Yes, sir," and got down on the floor.

***

The slow pace of his army crawl and the stretched latex's impairment of his vision caused Glont to make a few wrong turns, so that it took him ten minutes to get back to his cube. When at length he dragged himself up to his cube entrance, a blurry pair of legs ending in an equally blurry pair of floppy shoes stood mere inches from his face. Glont yanked the condom off his head with a snap.

"Dude," Sam the clown said, gawking down at Glont with a look of concern. "Did you hear the news yet?"

Glont pushed himself off the floor, slowly, as if he wished to stay down there—and he did. "What news?"

"About Fallingwater."

"No." Glont hadn't thought about the place in years.

"The barbed wire fence and all those KEEP OUT and NO TRESPASSING signs are gone. And the NO SWIMMING and NO KAYAKING signs along the creek—they're all gone, too. There's even a couple of canoes stacked on the streambank at that spot where everyone used to get into the creek."

"So?"

"Well? You know what that means, right?"

Glont thought about it for a beat before he put two and two together.

As a child, Ma Ruth had always taken Glont, Tom Two, and The Membrane out as a group on Halloween (Glont trick-or-treated at the same houses where Tom Two and The Membrane reverse trick-or-treated). That included Fallingwater. Some of his fondest childhood memories were of riding a canoe with his family on Bear Run at the end of Halloween night to see Old Man Cruthers' Halloween display, get one last handful of candy, and ride down the water slide. But then the Fallingwater tragedy occurred, and that was the end of that. Thereafter, Tom Two and The Membrane were no longer obligated to reverse trick-or-treat at Fallingwater because the new owner forbade all visitors.

But if the barbed wire fence and signs had been removed, that meant Tom Two and The Membrane would have to include Fallingwater in their reverse trick-or-treating itinerary once again.

"Shit." Glont shook his head, not wanting to believe it. "Who told you that?"

"A bunch of people here at work. I think pretty much everyone in town knows about it by now. Bob—you know, the dude who does jigsaw puzzles and smokes opium all day long?—he was the first to mention it to me when I got here this morning. He said he was down there hiking by the stream yesterday and saw for himself. Then Janet—you know, that chick who gets shitfaced every night and sleeps off her hangovers in her cube all day long every day?—she basically told me the same thing. She said she went into the woods last night to get blackout drunk and saw that all the signs were missing. Then after I talked to her, Brandon—

you know, the dude who chain-smokes and plays *GTA* in his dirty SpongeBob boxers all day long, he told me that—"

"Alright, alright, I get it. So the whole town probably knows about this."

"Yeah. So what are you gonna do?"

"Whaddaya mean, what am I gonna do? I'm gonna take my 'phews reverse trick-or-treating like I do every year. I guess we'll just have to hit Fallingwater this time. Hey, if the barbed wire fence and the signs are gone, I imagine others are gonna go out there too, right?" Glont gulped nervously.

"I don't think so, man. I'm pretty sure anyone who doesn't have to go out there won't be going out there. I mean, who the hell would wanna go to that place with the possibility of TERROR MANNEQUIN lurking there? No parent is gonna want to take their kids trick-or-treating there."

"TERROR MANNEQUIN was probably just some asshole in a costume," Glont said with uncertainty. "Whoever he was, there's no reason to believe he's still out there thirty years later. TERROR MANNEQUIN is just a story told to scare kids."

"What if it's not just a story? What if TERROR MANNEQUIN is a real demonic entity that still haunts Fallingwater after all these years, waiting for people to come back so it can bust out its jack-in-the-box on their asses?"

"You're an idiot. Regardless, I have to take Tom Two and The Membrane out there tomorrow night. If I don't, the town will lynch them."

"But you don't have to go with them. Why not just put them in a canoe by themselves, send them on their way, and hope for the best?"

Glont grabbed Sam by the collar of his clown suit, shook him. "Fuck you, Bozo. You're talking about my 'phews, dude. You think I'm just gonna send them in there by themselves if it could be dangerous?"

Sam pulled away from Glont's grasp. "Easy, man. Just lookin' out for you, is all. I mean, *if* TERROR MANNEQUIN is still there, there's no sense in all three of you dying, right?"

"Fuck you," Glont said as he left Sam and entered his cubicle. A moment after he collapsed into his recliner, his desk phone rang. Reluctantly, he picked it up. "Yellllo, this is Glont."

"Glont. It's Lance Montgomery."

Shit, Glont thought, his head sinking. "Hello, Mr. Montgomery."

"Hey, I forgot to mention something when I spoke to you earlier. I'm gonna need you to go down to the courthouse tomorrow morning and have your name legally changed from Glont Lamont to My Tiny Little Weak Bitch, m'kay."

"Whu-whu-what?"

"Are you deaf, shithead?"

"No, sir. It's just that, um, I kind of like my name. There's, like, really no reason to change it."

"What you like or don't like doesn't matter, you turd-jugglin' retard. Go down to the courthouse tomorrow morning and have your name legally changed to My Tiny Little Weak Bitch or you're fucking fired. Capiche?"

Glont mustered a sudden burst of courage. "Go ahead and fire me, you dumb, steroid-eatin', meathead, trust fund bro. I hate this job anyway. You wanna fuck with me, Lance? Come at me, bro. I'll stab you in your fuckin' face, you blowhard asshole!"

"Oooooo-eeeeee, look at Mr. Brave Man—finally sticking up for himself after all these years! Well, how about that shit? Hey, if you want me to fire you, I'll fucking fire you. But then what are you gonna do about that big ol' house you can't afford to live in, eh? What are you gonna do about that freak family of yours? Are you just gonna pick up and leave town like your deadbeat dad did? And what about those expensive medications your loathsome old, bag-of-bones mother needs? Because I know for a fact that no one else is hiring in town except for maybe Taco Hell, and you and I both know you can't pay your bills making minimum wage."

Glont knew Lance was right. He closed his eyes, hung his head in defeat, took a deep breath, and said, "I'm very sorry for my outburst, sir. No, I don't want to be fired."

"That's what I thought, My Tiny Little Weak Bitch. Apology accepted. Now, do what I said and make that trip to the courthouse tomorrow morning, m'kay?"

"Yes, Mr. Montgomery."

Chapter 8

"Did ya hear 'bout Fallingwater?" Ma Ruth asked the moment Glont entered the front door.

"Yeah, I heard," Glont said dejectedly. He shut the door behind him, hung his jacket on the coat rack, and turned to face her. Sitting in her rocker, his mother wore a rubber Freddy Krueger mask—an expensive one by the looks of it—and what appeared to be a homemade Freddy Krueger glove constructed from an old work glove and four steak knives.

"Wow, Ma. That's a pretty great getup. I didn't know you were dressing up for Halloween this year. That Freddy mask is amazing. In fact, you look more like Freddy Krueger than Freddy Krueger does. Did you order it on Amazon? You better not have spent a lot of money on that."

"I ain't spent no money at all, boy. It's not a mask."

"Whaddaya mean it's not a mask."

"It's not a mask. I decided to be Freddy fer Halloween this year, and I knew we couldn't afford a mask. So earlier today, I filled the kitchen sink with water, went out to the garage with some matches, doused my head with gasoline, and set it afire. Then I ran back inside, screamin' bloody murder, dunked my head into the sink to put out the flames. It hurt a good bit, but it worked real good, huh?" Ma Ruth raised the clawed glove in the air while she imitated Freddy's diabolical laughter.

"Jesus Christ, Ma! Look what you did to yourself! Are you in pain right now?"

"Nah. As long as I keep smokin' this clown tear-laced meth I got, I'll be alright." She gestured at a glass pipe sitting on the end table beside her, its bulbous end scorched black. "I feel jus' fine."

"But you're disfigured now! Severely and permanently. And all your hair is gone! Is that what you wanted?"

"Sure is. Y'know what a fan o' Freddy I am." The woman cackled at the alliteration and near rhyming of her remark, repeating it in crazed singsong: "Fan o' Freddy I am! Fan o' Freddy I am! Fan o' Freddy I am! Fan o' Freddy I am! Har-har-har-har…"

"Ma, I think we should take you to the hospital. Burns that bad can become infected."

"Nah, I'll be okay. If it looks like they're startin' to get 'fected, I'll just pour some salt on 'em. Or some mercury. Maybe put leeches on 'em. I can also cauterize 'em some more with a blowtorch if need be. And if none of that helps, I can always give myself a frontal lobotomy."

Glont shook his head in bafflement. "If you say so, Ma. Did you tell Tom Two and The Membrane about Fallingwater yet?"

"Nah. I was going to, but they ran upstairs when they saw my new Freddy face."

Glont crossed the living room to the hall and called up the stairs: "Hey, you two. Come on down here. I need to talk to you. And don't be scared of Ma Ruth. She's just dressed up for Halloween." He went back into the living room, sat on the couch.

Tom Two and The Membrane came down a minute later, slogged into the room, both looking glum.

"Come up here, Double T," Glont said as he patted the sofa cushion next to him. Tom Two did as he was told, climbing up onto the sofa and sitting right up against Glont's leg. Glont put his arm around him while The Membrane settled by his feet.

"Hey, Tom. Don't be afraid of your crazy, old Ma Ruth. She just made herself look like Freddy for Halloween, is all. Well, Halloween and all the other days in the year, I guess. Still, nothing to be scared of."

Tom Two shook his head and signed a response: *It's not her I'm scared of.*

"Okay. Well, what are you scared of then?"

Tom Two signed again: *TERROR MANNEQUIN!*

"TERROR MANNEQUIN? Well, that's what I wanted to talk to you guys about. What do you know about TERROR MANNEQUIN, Tom Two?"

Tom Two indicated he knew the whole story behind TERROR MANNEQUIN. He also knew that he and The Membrane would have to go reverse trick-or-treating at Fallingwater tomorrow. Apparently, The Membrane had snuck out late last night after everyone had gone to bed, as it was wont to do on occasion. The thing went to play at the nearby community park, where it happened upon some teenagers drinking on the playground. While spying on them, it heard them talking about how Tom Two and The Membrane would have to go reverse trick-or-treating at Fallingwater this year or else they would get lynched by the townspeople.

The teenagers also said that TERROR MANNEQUIN was there waiting for them.

Glont cast The Membrane a look of a disapproval. "Well, you're lucky no one caught you last night. Because if they had, they could have killed you. Yes, we have to go to Fallingwater tomorrow night for reverse trick-or-treat. We haven't had to do that in many years because of the barbed wire fence and the signs telling everyone to keep out, but now the signs and the fence are gone. That much is true.

"But this TERROR MANNEQUIN business? It's probably just all made up. There's no proof that TERROR MANNEQUIN is real. There's definitely no proof TERROR MANNEQUIN is still at Fallingwater, waiting for a fresh batch of victims."

The Membrane formed two arm-like appendages and signed at Glont: *But we also can't be sure that TERROR MANNEQUIN isn't real.*

"You're right. We don't know for sure that TERROR MANNEQUIN is *not* real, and that TERROR MANNEQUIN is *not* skulking around Fallingwater right now as we speak, waiting to kill again. That's why I want to leave the decision to go there to you guys. If you don't go, you know the townspeople will kill you or drive you out of town. So we can do one of two things. We can take our chances and go reverse trick-or-treating at Fallingwater and just hope for the best. Or you guys can skip town. We can hop in the car and drive far, far away from Selohssa. I can take you guys to a new city, maybe some place where the people are friendlier, a place where you can both make a fresh start. There's a little town in southern Ohio called Chillville where everyone is chill as hell. Assholes aren't even allowed to live in Chillville.

Maybe we could go there. Or maybe I can take you out into the wilderness, somewhere safe and secluded, and we could build a cabin for you guys to live in, set you up with a generator. I couldn't live there with you—I have to stay here and take care of Ma Ruth, but I'd drive out to visit as often as I could, bring you fuel and supplies and whatnot—SpaghettiOs with meatballs, Totino's Party Pizzas, horror movies, games, and whatever else you needed. Whaddya think?"

Tom Two signed back, indicating he wanted to take his chances and go reverse trick-or-treating at Fallingwater. He said he didn't want to live anywhere in the world except in the Lamont family ancestral home—that he didn't want to go anywhere else if Glont, Ma Ruth, and The Membrane didn't go with him.

"How about you?" Glont asked The Membrane. "You feel the same way?"

The Membrane signed back, indicating that it wished it was a tall, handsome, musclebound, big-dicked man so it could get mad amounts of ass and geyser-gush gallons of trouser gravy all over hot sluts' faces.

"Hey, I know you want to get mad amounts of ass and geyser-gush gallons of trouser gravy all over hot sluts' faces, but that's not what we're fucking talking about right now, is it? Stay on topic. So, are you cool with going out to Fallingwater tomorrow night or not?"

The Membrane sprouted a fat, balloon-like thumb at the end of one of its limbs and made a thumbs up.

Chapter 9

Late in the morning the following day found Glont seated in a chair before the clerk of courts, one Laura Higgins, a prim-looking, full-figured, thirtyish woman who sat opposite him at her desk in the Selohssa district courthouse, her blonde and copper-highlighted hair sculpted in a sweeping "I'd Like To Speak to Your Manager" hairdo.

She flipped through the thick packet of forms he'd just filled out and handed to her, making sure each was complete. When she came to the line where he'd neatly printed his new name, she furrowed her brow in puzzlement.

"My Tiny Little Weak Bitch," she read slowly, crinkling her nose. "Is that really what you want to change your name to, Mr. Lamont?"

"No, of course I don't want to. But if I don't, I'll be fired from my job."

The clerk smirked, shook her head in amazement. "Well, okay. Let's get this taken care of then." She proceeded to notarize the forms by stamping, dating, and adding her signature to each one. She talked while she worked.

"I know who you are, ya know. You're the Glont Lamont who lives with those two fucking freaks."

Glont was not impressed. He sat with his arms folded across his chest, head slightly tipped to the side, staring right through the woman's face as if she wasn't there while waiting for her to finish.

Speaking through clenched teeth, the clerk said, "God, how I hate Tom Two and The Membrane! God, how I wish they'd both just fucking die already and burn in hell for eternity!"

Unfazed, Glont didn't so much as blink in response.

"Well, considering that you take care of those two monsters, I suppose you kinda deserve your new name. I mean, it just sorta serves you right."

After the clerk stamped the last form in the packet, she rose from her chair to make copies in the machine behind her. "Now it's official," she said while handing him his copies. "That'll be one-hundred and fifty dollars, Mr. Lamont—oops!—I mean, My Tiny Little Weak Bitch. Tee-hee-hee!"

Glont—oops, I mean My Tiny Little Weak Bitch—handed over the cash, and the clerk gave him a receipt.

"Bye-bye, My Tiny Little Weak Bitch!" the clerk said, bursting into a fit of hysterical laughter.

Papers in hand, Glont trudged to the open doorway, where he halted and stood still for a moment before turning back around to face the clerk. "Ya know what?" he asked.

"What, My Tiny Little Weak Bitch?" the woman asked, laughing again.

"Even if you were to lose fifty pounds and get a nosejob, you'd still only be about a 5.5."

Shocked into silence, the clerk's eyes bulged in their sockets. "Why, I never! You…you…your dick's a 5.5!" That was the best comeback she could come up with.

"Yeah, 5.5 inches of motherfuckin' *limp* dick," Glont lied as he turned to leave.

Chapter 10

After he left the courthouse, My Tiny Little Weak Bitch—let's just call him "Weak Bitch" for short, shall we?—decided he didn't want to go to work. He was sure news of his new name had already spread around the office, and he wasn't quite ready to be taunted about it there. Instead, he drove to the grocery store to buy reverse trick-or-treating candy and treats for the Halloween afterparty he, Tom Two, and The Membrane would have later that night. He filled a shopping cart with bags of Snickers, Twix, Kit Kats, Skittles, Nestle's Nursing Homes, Hershey's Hospices, and Cadbury Crème-atoriums, as well as cookies, caramel apples, and apple cider for the party.

A smirking, zit-faced teenage boy named Pete Perkins rang up and bagged his groceries. Just as Weak Bitch walked away from the checkout counter with a plastic grocery bag dangling from each hand, Pete said, "Happy Halloween, My Tiny Little Weak Bitch!" He punctuated the gibe with a snicker.

Weak Bitch stopped, stared straight ahead for a beat, did an about-face. "Wow. Word about my new name is spreading faster than I thought. Well, whatever. It is what it is, I guess. Happy Halloween to you, too, pizza face. I hope you get horrible, permanent acne scars that turn into skin cancer."

The kid's smirk deflated into a frown.

"Oh, and by the way," Weak Bitch added. "I know who you are, Pete. Your mom is Sally Perkins. I briefly dated her in high school. Well, I guess we never technically dated, but I did fuck her in the ass once and blow a big, goopy gob of trouser gravy all over her long-ass, ugly, zit-covered horseface. Well, I gotta get going. I hope you and everyone you hold dear get aggressive forms of cancer, leprosy, bubonic plague, and early-onset Alzheimer's."

***

When Weak Bitch arrived back home, Ma Ruth was in her rocker knitting herself a green and red striped Freddy Krueger sweater. An old, dusty fedora that she'd found somewhere in the house sat atop her toasted head.

"Seven or eight people called this mornin' lookin' fer someone named My Tiny Little Weak Bitch," she said. "I kept tellin' 'em they had the wrong number, but they'd jus' laugh at me."

"They were calling for me, Ma. I went down to the courthouse today to get my name changed to My Tiny Little Weak Bitch this morning."

"Well, whaddya go and do a fool thing like that for, boy?"

"I had to. Lance Montgomery said he'd fire me from Fun 4-Life if I didn't."

"Oh, that Lance Montgomery. Still givin' ya a hard time after all these years. He sure is a handsome one, though! Big n' strong. And that dandy bulge in his trousers is somethin' else! Tee-hee-hee!"

"Jesus Christ," Weak Bitch muttered, shaking his head. He left her to put away the groceries.

"Hey, don't forget to hitch Tom Two's wagon to the back of my scooter today. Ya hear me, My Tiny Little Weak Bitch? Tee-hee-hee!"

Chapter 11

A group of costumed children dashed up the driveway of the house directly across the street from the Lamont residence while Mr. and Mrs. Brown, the owners of the house, sat in patio chairs placed near an iron fire pit where a few split birch logs burned low and orange, spicing the crisp, cool, autumnal air—air that already smelled of dry leaves—with redolent woodsmoke, while a gaggle of glowing jack-o'-lanterns grinned behind them on the front steps.

"Trick-or-treat!" the children called out in chorus.

"Oh, look at you all! A ninja, a T-Rex, a skeleton, a football player, and a princess!" Mrs. Brown said. She was dressed in a long black dress and a pointy black witch's hat.

"I'm Belle from *Beauty and the Beast*," the little girl corrected her.

"Ah, Belle! Well, of course you are! How precious!"

Mrs. Brown reached into a plastic cauldron filled with fun-sized Snickers, Milky Ways, Milk Duds, Nestle's Crunch, Nestle's Nursing Homes, Hershey's Hospices, and Cadbury Crème-atoriums. She dropped candy into the children's bags.

Each child dutifully said, "Thank you," after she gave them their candy, except for the little four-year-old skeleton, who turned to run back down the driveway, forgetting his manners and overeager to get to the next house.

He only made it a few steps before his father's large hand intercepted him.

"Did you forget to say something, Bobby?" his dad said as he grasped the boy gently by the shoulders and turned him back toward the Browns.

"Thank you!" the boy's peanut voice shrilled.

Mr. and Mrs. Brown both laughed. "You're very welcome!" Mrs. Brown said. "Happy Halloween, kids!"

Back on the sidewalk, the adults steered their kids away from the next small group waiting to walk up the Brown's driveway: Tom Two, The Membrane, and Weak Bitch. Tom Two led the way with The Membrane creeping along right behind him. The two-year-old bore a candy-stuffed pillowcase over his shoulder, making him look like some tiny, disfigured Santa Claus while The Membrane conveyed its bag of candy atop its flat, pancake-like body. Weak Bitch followed several steps behind them.

Grinning ear to ear only seconds ago, Mr. and Mrs. Brown's faces contorted into haughty sneers as soon as the couple saw the town's only reverse trick-or-treaters coming up their driveway. Tom Two halted before the cauldron of candy, plopped his pillowcase on the concrete in front of him, and gave the Brown's a friendly wave, a gesture that was not reciprocated. He reached into the sack, extracted a Milky Way and a roll of Smarties, dropped them into the cauldron.

"Fuck you, Tom Two," Mr. Brown hissed. "God, how I fucking hate you!"

"Why, I'll smack your little face, Tom Two!" Mrs. Brown said, the woman's bottom lip trembling with atavistic rage.

She would do no such thing, of course, and everyone there knew it. They could talk all they wanted, but so long as Tom Two and The Membrane carried out their civic duty of reverse trick-or-treating once a year, no one was allowed to lay a finger on them.

The Browns watched with disgust as The Membrane edged forward, formed a crude limb from its body, reached into its bag, and dropped a few Tootsie Rolls into their cauldron.

"Fuck you, The Membrane," Mr. Brown said, spitting contemptuously on the ground in front of the thing. "You make me fucking sick!"

"You freaks!" Mrs. Brown hissed. "I wish you two abominations—you monsters!—would just die already!"

"Yeah, fuck you too, bitch," Weak Bitch said. "People like you are the real monsters. Let's go, guys."

The forgiving little bastard that he was, Tom Two waved bye-bye to the couple before he slung his candy sack over his shoulder and turned to leave, the back of his sombrero dragging on the ground behind him. Far less polite, The Membrane formed a balloon-like middle finger at the end of a limb and thrust it forward for the couple to feast their eyes on, before following Tom Two and Weak Bitch back to the sidewalk and to the next house.

Nobody was home next door, but the front porchlight was on and a bowl had been placed on the doormat to receive the boys' reverse trick-or-treat offerings. That's what people in Selohssa did when they weren't going to be home on Halloween night. Also, such absentees usually left messages for Tom Two and The Membrane. Taped to the door of this particular house was a piece of paper with the words

"FUCK YOU, TOM TWO AND THE MEMBRANE! DIE! DIE! DIE!" written on it with a marker.

These were the easy houses—the houses where no one was home. And every year, Weak Bitch wished there were more of them—houses where his 'phews didn't have to listen to people's cruel bullshit. But there were never enough of those.

The next house they stopped at was the home of Russ Robinson, the town's miserable alcoholic dogcatcher. After Tom Two rang the doorbell, the gaunt, drunken, mid-fiftyish man appeared at the screen door, a can of Natty Daddy gripped in one hand, a lit Marlboro in the other, his jowly, grizzled, five-o'-clock-shadowed face glowering down at them. "Well, look at you two fuckers."

Tom Two gave the man a friendly wave, to which Russ responded, "Boy, you two are some of the ugliest-lookin' sumbitches I ever seen. And you'se not even wearing costumes! Heh." Grinning smugly, the man sipped at his beer as he swayed drunkenly in place, not moving to open the door. "Hey, I bet you two are fags, too. Heh-heh." He took another gulp of ND, followed by a pull on his cigarette.

"You want your candy or not, Russ?" Weak Bitch asked from the bottom of the stoop.

Russ chuckled. "Why don'tcha mind yer own damn business, My Tiny Little Weak Bitch."

"This is my damn business. These boys don't have to wait here any longer than a minute for you to accept their offering. That's the rule."

"I knows the goddamn rules! But my minute's not up yet. Heh! Hey, Tom Two—you do know that TERROR

MANNEQUIN's gonna git ya tonight out at Fallingwater, right? Heh-heh!"

Tom Two, who held out a fun-sized Twix for the man, dropped his eyes fearfully to the ground.

Weak Bitch quickly ascended the steps. "Go ahead and drop the candy right there on the porch, Tom Two. You too, The Membrane. This scumbag's taking too damn long."

They did as their uncle told them.

"I'll take as long as I goddamn want, ya pole smokers!"

"Yeah, that hurts a lot comin' from somebody whose job it is to drive around drunk all day long searching for stray puppies to murder. Let's roll, fellas."

"Hey, you can't talk to me like that!" the man said as he finally opened the door, stumbling out onto the stoop. "Why, I was elected dogcatcher by the goddamn townspeople! I'm a goddamn vet, ya faggots! Why, I fought the A-rabs in the Gulf War, ya yellow-bellied pansies! I…"

"Ignore that TERROR MANNEQUIN talk, Tom Two," Weak Bitch said as he walked beside Tom Two down the driveway. "That asshole doesn't know what the hell he's talking about. We'll be just fine."

"And one more thing," the tottering dogcatcher called out into the night as the trio crossed the street, leaving him behind:

"Fuuuuck yoooouuuuuuu, Tom Twooooooooooo-ooooooooooooooooooooooooooooooooooooooooooo ooooooooooo!!!!"

***

While trick-or-treating in Selohssa lasted from 6:00 PM to 9:00 PM, reverse trick-or-treating usually lasted from 6:00 PM to about 10:00 PM. That's because it took Tom Two and company about four hours to work their way through the working-class south side of town and then hit all the houses in the more well-to-do north side. As far as the sort of treatment they encountered each and every year, their stops at Russ Robinson's and the Browns' were par for the course: the cruel jeering, taunting laughter, finger pointing, the faces pinched in mixed expressions of varying degrees of revulsion, hatred, anger, and fear. On the sidewalks, trick-or-treaters invariably gave the trio a wide berth as if they were lepers. And although some people leered silently at the trio as they passed them by on the sidewalk, most folks felt compelled to get in at least a dig or two.

Many of the insults directed at them were recited and repeated word-for-word throughout the town. Over the decades, the townspeople developed several favorite taunts and invectives that they passed down from generation to generation so that certain regular iterations of cruelty and abuse became part of the reverse trick-or-treating tradition.

Of course, "Fuck you, Tom Two!" and "I hate you, Tom Two!" had always been in wide use, but so had "Why, I'll smack your little hand, Tom Two!" and "Why, I'll pinch your little arm, Tom Two!" Other phrases that had gained popularity in the past decade were "I just want to light you on fucking fire, The Membrane, then shove you straight up Tom Two's little ass!" and "Why, I'll rip your fucking face off, Tom Two, and stretch The Membrane over your screaming, bloody skull to make you a new face!"

On the other hand, young children were taught slurs of a less violent and more G-rated nature, such as "Why, I'll step on your shoe, Tom Two!" and "Tom Two is a bad boy!" and "You be quiet, Tom Two!" and "The Membrane is nothing but a big, stinky pancake!"

It all sounds pretty awful, but Tom Two and The Membrane had been doing this for so long now that they no longer cared what people said about them. The last time anyone had managed to make Tom Two cry had been three generations ago, back when the task of escorting them around town on Halloween night had belonged to Weak Bitch's great grandfather. But this year was different because comments about TERROR MANNEQUIN were now mixed in with all those tired, old chestnuts. Also, intermingled here and there among all those faces expressing the usual feelings of anger, disgust, and hatred were looks of quasi-sympathetic solemnity—the type of facial expressions people normally reserved for those condemned to death.

Still, the whole phenomenon was relatively safe regardless of how fucked up it was. Over the years, Tom Two and The Membrane had never been seriously assaulted by any of the townspeople during reverse trick-or-treating despite the threats of violence involved in the practice. However, minor incidents occurred on occasion, usually involving children who didn't know any better.

Case in point: on this particular Halloween, after visiting about one-third of the houses on the north side of town, the trio encountered a boy of about eight or nine who was dressed up as Chucky from *Child's Play*. He was with his little sister, a kindergartener dressed as Miley Cyrus (complete with a plastic sledgehammer for lascivious licking).

Their mother, one Sharon Simmons—an uppity-looking, sour-faced, she-bitch of a woman—accompanied them. While people generally moved out of their way on the sidewalk, these folks blocked their path and refused to move.

"Why, I'll smack your little hand, Tom Two!" Sharon said.

The woman's slutty little Miley Cyrus-with-a-sledgehammer daughter followed that up with, "Why, I'll step on your toe, Tom Two!"

"Just move out of their way," Weak Bitch said to his nephews, "and walk on the grass, guys."

Tom Two did as Weak Bitch said, sidestepping onto the tree lawn to go around the hateful trick-or-treaters.

Gripping a long, thick stick he'd picked up off the sidewalk moments ago, the boy dressed as Chucky said, "Why, I'll smart you on your knee with this stick, Tom Two!"

The sincerity of the kid's tone made Weak Bitch a little nervous. "Hey, Sharon," he said. "Keep your friggin' kids in line, okay?"

"Don't you talk to me, you south side Lamont scum!"

As Tom Two passed the boy, he wound the stick back and swung hard, aiming for Tom Two's knee, but Tom Two was quick enough to use his candy bag as a shield to block the blow.

Weak Bitch snatched the stick from the kid's hands. Turning to face the mother, he gripped it in both hands like a samurai sword, wound back, and shook with rage as his glaring eyes locked with hers.

"Go ahead," she said.

Other trick-or-treaters and parents pressed in on both sides of the confrontation, curious to see what was going on.

"Go ahead and swing at me, My Tiny Little Weak Bitch," the mother said, smiling sardonically, "and you'll be spending the rest of your Halloween in a fucking jail cell."

Weak Bitch held her gaze for another moment, imagining the satisfaction of breaking the stick over her head, but after exhaling a deep breath, he tossed it into the street. The trio then moved on.

Chapter 12

Luckily for our reverse trick-or-treaters, not everyone in town was a complete blithering asshole. In fact, a few Selohssa residents actually supported and pitied Tom Two and The Membrane. Despite their sympathy and their deep disapproval of the cruel practice of reverse trick-or-treating, these individuals were bound by law to receive reverse trick-or-treating candy on Halloween just like everyone else. And these folks were forbidden to give Tom Two and The Membrane Halloween candy, however much they might wish to ease the boys' misery just a bit by doing so. In fact, giving candy or any other gifts to Tom Two and The Membrane on Halloween night was an offense punishable by death. As such, a Selohssa resident could never be sure there wasn't someone hiding in their front bushes or behind a nearby tree, someone who'd been tasked to follow Tom Two and The Membrane around all night long, someone just waiting to catch a sympathetic person in the illicit act of slipping Tom Two a piddly-ass lollipop or something.

But no rules existed to prevent the few kindhearted individuals in town from offering Tom Two and The Membrane hugs and words of encouragement.

Django Ferdinando was one such individual.

But before I go ahead and describe Django Ferdinando at great length and in meticulous detail—i.e., all the man's hopes, dreams, strengths, scruples, virtues, fears, accomplishments, flaws, failures, likes, dislikes, beliefs, habits, and idiosyncrasies; the childhood spent in the gypsy caravans of Eastern Europe; the young adulthood experienced as a clown in the Satanic traveling circuses of Central Europe; the years spent in France as a fancy-pants, artsy-fartsy, beret-wearing fancy dude; the years employed as a cloaked Illuminati assassin in the Far East; the harrowing, nearly fatal transatlantic voyage to the Americas via sea kayak; the years spent in Canada as a lumberjack/crab fisherman/ice road trucker; nay, before I proceed to tell this man's whole goddamn life story, I'd just like to remark briefly on the correction pronunciation of his name.

Which is to say I would simply like to point out that the "D" in Django is silent.

Oh, wait a second. Now that I think about it, the "j" is silent too.

Hm. Now that I think about it even more, it appears the "a" is also not pronounced.

Whoa. Upon even more thought on this subject, I must note that the "n" in Django is silent as well.

And the "g."

And the "o."

What's more, and as odd as it may seem, if we are to properly enunciate the man's full name, we must also refuse to pronounce the "F" in Ferdinando.

And believe it or not, the "e" following the silent "F" is just as silent!

As is the "r" and the "d" and the "i" and the "n" and the "a" and the second "n" and the second "d" and the final "o."

Of course, what all this means is that the man's entire name is silent!

But that can't be right.

Can it?

Shit. Now I'm confused.

Hm...

Hm...

Oh, now I remember! The reason Django Ferdinando's name is completely silent is (drumroll please)...

BECAUSE THERE IS NO DJANGO FERDINANDO!

You wanna know why? Well, remember when I claimed earlier in this chapter that not everyone in town was a complete blithering asshole? That there were also good people who supported Tom Two and The Membrane?

I LIED!

Why the hell would I lie about that?

Man, I don't even know. Maybe I just wanted to pretend, if only for a moment, that things weren't as bad in Selohssa as they actually were.

Because basically EVERYONE IN FUCKING TOWN was a COMPLETE BLITHERING, BLATHERING, BLUSTERING FUCKING ASSHOLE! So sorry for the contradictory information presented earlier in this chapter and any confusion it may have caused.

And if you doubt me at all about the incredible amount of assholery that gripped the little burgh of Selohssa, Pennsylvania, just take a look at what "Selohssa" spells backwards, yo!

Humph!

>:(

Chapter 13

When the trio approached Lance Montgomery's mansion on the sidewalk of Diamond Boi Drive, the time was a quarter till ten, and the boys' candy sacks were nearly empty. They had only a few houses to go. Though glad to be nearly done with reverse trick-or-treating for another year, Weak Bitch was filled with dread—dread at still having to stop at Lance's place *and* Fallingwater. And he wasn't sure which stop he dreaded more.

As they turned off the sidewalk and passed through the stone pillars and tall iron gate at the end of the house's long driveway, Weak Bitch hoped this would be one of those years where Lance was too busy partying to come out to harass them, usually by daring Weak Bitch to try a BigBoy XXL on for size in front of a jeering crowd of drunken guests, but he knew that was probably asking for too much.

Two and a half acres of well-groomed lawn lay to the right of the car-lined driveway, while a row of tall, closely planted pine trees flanked the left side. Closer to the house, the driveway divided into a circle that led in either direction to the mansion's Doric-columned portico. When the group reached the broad stone steps that led up to the front door, they peered into the house through the high, lighted windows of the front façade, the curtains drawn, the rooms overflowing with costumed guests, the windowpanes vibrating with the bumping bass of shitty dance-pop music.

The Membrane formed its limbs and signed up at Weak Bitch: *Hey, that naughty nurse just flashed her tits!*

"Don't look, Tom Two," Weak Bitch said, covering Tom Two's eyes with one hand.

Why not? I'm eons old! Tom Two signed.

"Enough peeping already. Ring the doorbell, Tom Two."

A few seconds after Tom Two did so, a butler answered the door. He looked from Tom Two to The Membrane to Weak Bitch.

"Go ahead, guys," Weak Bitch said. "Give him some candy. Then we'll get going."

"One moment, sirs. Please wait here," the butler said before stepping back and pulling the door shut after him.

Fucking great, Weak Bitch thought.

When the door opened again a moment later, Lance Montgomery stepped out onto the portico accompanied by a small entourage of partygoers, among them Amanda, who was dressed up as a Sexy Little Red Riding Hood. She averted her eyes when she saw Weak Bitch.

Dressed as a king—complete with a long wine-colored robe, jeweled crown, and golden scepter—Lance handed the scepter to one of his frat boy buddies before crouching down in front of Tom Two.

"Hail, little fellow," Lance said in a bad British accent delivered with an uncharacteristically friendly tone of voice and a broad smile. He patted Tom Two lightly on the head.

Tom Two waved back.

"Art thou having a fun Halloween so far, Sir Two?"

Tom Two nodded, smiling at being called "Sir Two."

"Well, I'm glad to hear it," Lance said.

Tom Two reached into his bag, pulled out a lollipop, held it out to Lance.

"Thank thee," Lance said as he took the candy.

Weak Bitch watched this entire exchange with scorn, knowing this friendly bit was just a ruse, one that would end any second now—a cruel prelude to whatever manner of bullying Lance had planned for them tonight.

The Membrane slid up next to Tom Two and offered Lance a fun-sized Milky Way. Again, Lance accepted the gift. "And thank thee as well, Sir Membrane. Oh, that I could return the gesture by giving the two of thee some candy of thine own, but as thou knowest, the rules doth forbid it. I do, however, wish all three of thee a very happy and safe Halloween."

Lance stood, took his scepter back in one gloved hand, and placed his other hand on his hip, affecting some sort of regal pose. "Thou art free to go now," he said.

There's no way this is gonna be that easy, Weak Bitch thought. He looked uncertainly down at Tom Two, then at The Membrane, and back up at Lance, who continued to stand on the portico, a kingly statue, his costumed entourage gathered around him and almost eerily silent.

"Okay, guys," Weak Bitch said. "Let's get going."

The trio turned to leave, doubling back down the driveway. *Well, maybe it* is *going to be this easy*, Weak Bitch thought.

When they reached the point where the circle driveway merged into a straight path, Weak Bitch glanced over his shoulder. The group was still on the portico, a tableau with a faux king at its center, apparently content to watch them as they receded toward the street. He faced forward again and fixed his eyes on the open gate at the end of the driveway, watching the gate grow larger as the distance between it and him shrank.

"Let's speed it up, guys," Weak Bitch said, quickening his step. Seconds later, he looked over his shoulder again. The group remained at the entrance, perhaps waiting for him and his nephews to completely disappear from view. Ten paces later and they were nearly at the end of the drive. Weak Bitch glanced back one more time: the group still lingered at the entrance.

He turned back around just as they were about to pass between the two stone pillars, but the moment his foot crossed into the space beyond the gate, Lance screamed through cupped hands: "Halt, thee, My Little Tiny Weak Bitch!"

Fuck, Weak Bitch thought, stopping just outside the gate, reluctantly turning around.

"Get thee back here, knave!"

Weak Bitch started back down the driveway, his step quick, with Tom Two and The Membrane struggling to keep up with him. They stopped about halfway back to the house.

"Sorry, but your one minute is way over," Weak Bitch shouted. "That's the rule. We're outta here."

"Oh, I don't care about those two freaks and reverse trick-or-treat. They can go on their merry fucking way for all I care. I said for *thee* to get back here! Get back here now or thou art fired!"

***

Once again, Weak Bitch stood at the bottom of Lance's front steps, Tom Two and The Membrane now cowering behind him.

"I know I dismissed thee before," Lance said, "but then I remembered I needed thee to do me a little favor." Lance pointed his scepter down at Weak Bitch in a gesture of condemnation. "Namely, I need thee to bite off thy bottom lip, peasant! Do so now, My Tiny Little Weak Bitch!"

Lance's friends laughed.

"Wh-wh-what?" Weak Bitch blurted. "Is that even possible?"

"Thou shalt address me as *Your Majesty*, ye rapscallion! And, yes, of course it's possible. Just bite down really, really hard. If thou really want to keep thy job so thou can keep thy house, feed and shelter thy family of freaks, and pay for thy mother's medicines, I imagine a great deal is possible!"

Amanda appeared at the front of the crowd. "Don't do it, Glont!" she cried.

"His name is not Glont, wench." Lance said. "His name is My Tiny Little Weak Bitch. Now do as thy king hath biddeth, My Tiny Little Weak Bitch!"

"Yes, Your Majesty," Weak Bitch said. He turned to Amanda. "Sorry, but I have to do what he says."

Weak Bitch sucked his lower lip into his mouth—a warm, wet blanket of flesh pulling over his bottom teeth—and rested his top teeth on the other side. Pressing his eyes shut and bracing himself for the pain, he counted down in his head from five: *Five…four…three… two…ONE.*

A flash of blinding pain and the salty, metallic taste of blood filled his mouth. But he'd only barely broken the skin. Overcoming his mind's attempt to complete the painful act of self-mutilation, his body's automatic response was to pull its teeth away from its own flesh.

"I can't do it!" he cried.

"Surely thou canst! Oh, I almost forgot! Whilst thou art biting off thy bottom lip, pluck thine eyes out of thy face!" He waved the scepter at Weak Bitch again. "Do it now, ye villainous cur!"

After drawing his bleeding, abraded lower lip back into his mouth, Weak Bitch extended the thumb, index finger, and middle finger on each of his hands to form two three-fingered claws and raised them to his eyes. He counted down again in his head: *five…four…three…two…ONE.*

As the pain exploded in his lower lip, Weak Bitch dug into his eye sockets, his fingers and thumbs sliding beneath his eyelids to grab at his wet, slippery orbs while crimson tears of blood oozed down his cheeks.

In tears herself, Amanda seized Lance by the front of his robe and shouted into his face: "Make him stop or I'm leaving right now!"

Lance rolled his eyes, shook his head, and turned back to Weak Bitch. "Okay, fucker, you can stop now," he said, abandoning the British accent and the thee's and the thou's.

Weak Bitch released his mutilated lip from his teeth, his eyeballs from his fingers. He fell to his knees, his entire body shaking as he stared at his bloodied digits. But though his eyes hurt and his vision was blurry, he could still see.

"Do you do everything anyone tells you to?" Lance asked. "Christ, you were really going to gouge your eyes out and bite your lip off! Man, you need to grow a pair, bro. Heh.

What a gutless coward you are. Well, it's just as well, seeing as how I have better things to do than stand around out here and waste my time torturing useless, milquetoast geeks like you. I have to get back to my party, where I'm about to nab kingly amounts of ass. So gather up thy retarded abominations of nature and get thee far away from my castle, fags!"

Chapter 14

As they hit the last few houses on Diamond Boi Drive for reverse trick-or-treat, Weak Bitch held a hand over his mouth and chin, applying pressure to his lip in an attempt to stop the bleeding. He knew he probably needed stitches, but the boys had to wrap up reverse trick-or-treating by midnight or else be lynched by the townspeople. It was only a little past ten, but a trip to a potentially crowded ER was out of the question. He'd just have to keep applying pressure and hope for the best.

After they visited the last house on Diamond Boi, they made their way back to Klin-Klat Street at the southeastern end of town. Klin-Klat terminated in a dead end, where a footpath in the woods led down to a once-popular stretch of Bear Run where most visitors to Fallingwater used to enter the stream back in the day.

Weak Bitch could tell Tom Two and The Membrane were nervous as they entered the dark woods. He took out a flashlight and flicked it on.

"Alright, fellas," he said, his voice faking a lighthearted, enthusiastic tone for the benefit of his nephews lest he betray his own fear. "We're almost done. All we have left to do is enjoy ourselves on a little canoe trip, drop off the last of your candy at Fallingwater, then ride that old water slide out of the place. It'll be just like old times. After that, we'll go home and have our Halloween party!"

Not for the first time, Weak Bitch wondered how anyone in town would know if they even visited Fallingwater. Just because the KEEP OUT signs and the NO CANOEING signs and the barbed wire fence had all been removed didn't necessarily mean the mysterious, never-before-seen owner of the house was home. And if the owner was home, would they be waiting for trick-or-treaters and reverse trick-or-treaters alike? And even if they were, was the owner in contact with at least one other person in town, a person to whom the owner could pass on the message that Tom Two and The Membrane had or had not fulfilled their civic duty? There was a good chance the answer to that question was no. In other words, Tom Two, The Membrane, and Weak Bitch could possibly skip going out to Fallingwater altogether and say they reverse trick-or-treated at the place without anyone knowing any different.

But any last thoughts Weak Bitch entertained about taking their chances and not visiting Fallingwater were instantly dashed when he spotted his ex-girlfriend, Ma-He's-Makin'-Eyes-At-Me, standing next to the canoes that were stacked at the edge of stream bank.

Now in her late thirties, Ma-He's-Makin'-Eyes-At-Me Smith was a cursed woman who lived in a house at the end of Klin-Klat Street with her invisible monster of a mother. No one in town knew what the mother looked like, but many imagined Mrs. Smith as some sort of demonic clown-gorgon creature with sharks for arms, while other folks envisioned her as a hulking werewolf orbited by a school of zombie air-piranha. In any event, whenever Ma-He's-Makin'-Eyes-At-Me left her house, her mother always followed. Though no one ever actually saw Mrs. Smith, she was never far away from her daughter. She only made her invisible presence known when someone was hapless enough to look her daughter in the eye for more than a few seconds. If that happened, depending on the offender's gender, the daughter would either say, "Ma, he's makin' eyes at me!" or "Ma, she's makin' eyes at me!" in a sassy tattletale timbre, at which point the mother would come out of nowhere to pounce on the offender and tear them asunder. The daughter herself was not evil—she never wanted her mother to kill anyone—but the curse forced her to announce those fatal words of condemnation every time this happened.

No one had ever survived such an attack.

Weak Bitch and Ma-He's-Makin'-Eyes-At-Me had dated in high school towards the end of their senior year, and they'd gotten back together again for a few months when they were in their early twenties, but Weak Bitch had eventually broken up with her for good. For very understandable and practical reasons, dating the woman had proven too dangerous and stressful for him. But Ma-He's-Makin'-Eyes-At-Me still had feelings for Weak Bitch. Sometimes he'd look out his bedroom window at night and catch her standing out on the front sidewalk staring up at his house, all creeper-like.

"Hey, it's Ma-He's-Makin'-Eyes-At-Me," Weak Bitch said to Tom Two and The Membrane, just to make sure they saw her. He didn't need to give them any additional warning: they'd learned long ago to always look away from her face.

They stopped on the path, keeping her at a distance. As usual, the woman was dressed up as Dorothy from *The Wizard of Oz*, but not because it was Halloween. That was just her thing: she dressed up as Dorothy year-round. She even looked a bit like Judy Garland in the face.

"Um, hi," Weak Bitch said, looking down at the woman's ruby slippers. "It's been a long time."

"Yes, it has. How've you been, Glont?"

"Eh, I've been better. And my name's not Glont anymore actually. It's, er…My Tiny Little Weak Bitch."

"Yeah, I heard. Don't worry, you're still Glont to me." As usual, Ma-He's-Makin'-Eyes-At-Me was pleasant and polite. And unlike the rest of Selohssa's inhabitants, she'd never verbally harassed Tom Two or The Membrane, perhaps owing to her similar pariah-like status in the town.

"So," Weak Bitch said. "I'd ask you what you're doing here, but I'm guessing the Sheriff or someone else sent you to witness us reverse trick-or-treating at Fallingwater, right?"

"Actually, it was the mayor. But, yes. As I understand it, no one else really wanted to come out here to do it, but Mother and I don't mind at all."

Weak Bitch shuddered at the mention of her mother. "So what are you going to do?" he asked. "Ride in the canoe with us?"

"No. I'll ride in my own canoe and follow behind you. I'll keep my distance. I just need to see you float into the house, then mother and I can go home."

"Is, like, your mother going to ride in the canoe with you?"

"No. She'll be following along in the woods. She'll be watching you, too."

Weak Bitch, Tom Two, and The Membrane each peered fearfully into the wooded darkness surrounding them.

"You know, you really should at least say hello to her," Ma-He's-Makin'-Eyes-At-Me said. "Otherwise, she might take offense."

"Oh, yeah. Of course." Weak Bitch turned in place, waving to the woods in all directions. Tom Two and The Membrane followed his lead. "Hello, Mrs. Smith," Weak Bitch called out before gulping nervously. "I hope you're well, and that you're, um, having a nice Halloween."

He carried two canoes down to the stream in two separate trips, positioning them so they rested partly in the water. Tom Two and Ma-He's-Makin'-Eyes-At-Me each grabbed an oar from the pile next to the canoes. After the trio climbed into their canoe, Weak Bitch pushed off the streambank using the oar. Ma-He's-Makin'-Eyes-At-Me watched the current carry them downstream for a moment before she boarded her canoe.

A second after they got going, Weak Bitch and the boys heard a stick snap in the woods as the unseen beast commenced following them on the land.

Chapter 15

Weak Bitch had fond memories of Halloween in Selohssa, specifically the Halloweens prior to the tragedy at Fallingwater when his little family would wrap up the night by riding a canoe to the "Halloween castle in the woods," as many referred to the place back them.

He recalled that the house became visible after you floated around the first bend in the stream, appearing as a magical cluster of orange, purple, and green lights twinkling through the gaps in the trees—like a low-launched firework frozen mid-explosion. The shape of the building gradually materialized as the stream brought you closer to the lines, planes, and right angles of Fallingwater's asymmetrically stacked cantilevered floors and terraces, growing more definite as the distance shrank. Eventually, a recording of spooky Halloween sounds playing from speakers placed among the colored spotlights outside the house would reach your ears, heralding the final twist of the stream before Bear Run straightened out to lead directly into the arched entrance of the house's ground floor, which was usually decorated to resemble a great, yawning mouth.

However, after they drifted around the first bend in the stream on this particular night, there were no colorful lights twinkling in the woods to lure them further. Beyond the reach of the flashlight—which Tom Two gripped in both of his white-knuckled hands while directing its beam dead-ahead like a headlight—lay an inky darkness disrupted here and there by shafts of pale moonlight penetrating the canopy, as many of the tree branches still bore their soon-to-fall leaves, the light forming shimmering patches of silver on the water.

Seated at the stern of the canoe, Weak Bitch only occasionally dipped his oar in the water, mainly to keep the canoe from running aground while the stream's strong current did the rest of the work. Feeling tired and weak, he wanted to use the canoe ride as an opportunity to take a rest. Although he no longer tasted blood in his mouth, he was unaware of the slow but steady trickles of blood that continued to leak from his injured eyes and his mangled lip, rivulets that met at his chin before dripping down into his lap.

After a minute, Weak Bitch's sore eyes adjusted to the dark. The canoe passed between the point where the old barbed wire used to cross the stream. Barely visible in the gloom, one of the fence's end posts still stood alongside the streambank.

"See, guys," Weak Bitch said, "it's not so scary out here." However, he knew he didn't sound very convincing.

They floated onward into the darkness, the only sounds around them being the soft, white noise rush of the stream below them, the susurrant swish of wind through the tree branches above them, and the occasional solitary hoot of an owl. When the canoe reached the point on the stream where Weak Bitch remembered hearing the recorded Halloween sounds emanating from the house—ghoulish laughter, ghostly moans, rattling chains, werewolves howling, cauldrons bubbling, etc.—they still only heard the nightsounds of the woods.

The trees thinned out a beat later, Fallingwater's black shape looming into view against a stack of luminous clouds backlit by the moon. As the structure grew with their approach, the entrance to the basement took shape, an arched portal visible as a deeper shade of black painted on the surrounding darkness.

Weak Bitch was more afraid than he'd ever been in his life. It occurred to him that it wasn't too late for them to abandon ship—to climb out of the canoe and up the streambank, to run back the way they'd come. But was he even strong enough to make it back on foot? He was so tired, almost faint now.

But what was there for them to run back to?

His nephews' execution or exile, that's what.

When they were about twenty feet away from the portal, Weak Bitch set his oar beside him, content to let the current take them the rest of the way. "Looks like it's pitch black in there," he said. "I bet no one's home, which is perfectly fine by me. We'll float in, you guys will drop some candy on the ledge, and then we'll float right out the other side and down the slide. Easy peasy. Tom Two, gimme me the flashlight, will ya?"

Tom Two rose from his seat, clambered to the back of the canoe, dragging his nearly empty pillowcase with him. He handed the flashlight to Weak Bitch and climbed between his legs for protection, facing forward and peeking out through the gap that had formed between the brim of his sombrero and the edge of the seat, on which he rested his little hands. For its part, The Membrane curled into a ball and rolled next to Tom Two, trembling with fear.

"Aw, c'mon n-n-now," Weak Bitch said, his voice and hands shaking as he shone the flashlight dead ahead, its unsteady beam barely penetrating the dark gap that lay mere feet ahead of them. "There's n-n-nothing to be scared of here, b-b-boys."

Chapter 16

After they floated through the archway, Weak Bitch scanned the room quickly with the flashlight, his breathing short and heartbeat rapid as he swung the cone of light around the room like a lighthouse beacon. *Fuck all this helpless sitting around and waiting in dread bullshit*, he thought. If there was something waiting for them, he just wanted to see it already.

From what he saw, the room was empty. Back in happier times, when it wasn't Halloween and the weather was fair, Old Man Cruthers had used the ground floor of his house for entertaining guests. The basement-like chamber had been furnished with lounge furniture, billiard tables, televisions, stereo equipment, and a long wet bar with two shelves of liquor set against a mirrored wall and a polished marble countertop flanked by a dozen leather-wrapped stools. All those things were gone now. Instead, there was only the bare concrete expanse of floor, the sandstone and mortar walls, and the three evenly spaced concrete support columns. Stained here and there with blots and streaks of greenish-black mold, every visible surface sweated a patina of dampness that glistened in the flashlight's pale beam. Visible as a rectangle of brickwork, the former doorway to the staircase that lead up to the second floor had been sealed off with brick and mortar long ago.

No one else appeared to be in the room—either human or inhuman. However, the flashlight beam failed to reach behind the support columns. As such, Weak Bitch couldn't rule out the possibility that someone was hiding behind one of them.

The canoe bumped to a stop at the closed, mostly submerged swing gate that ran across the stream at about halfway across the chamber, the canoe's nose nudging between two of the dozen or so ring-shaped buoys tied to the top of the gate and floating atop the water.

"See, guys?" Weak Bitch asked uneasily, his still-bleeding eyes darting from one column to the next. "Nothing to be afraid of here. But let's hurry it up anyway. Go ahead and set some candy on the ledge."

Tom Two, still trembling with fear, climbed out from between his uncle's legs.

Fighting his mounting fatigue, Weak Bitch leaned to the side, reached out with his free hand, and grabbed the swing gate lever. "Hurry up. Then I'll pull the lever, and we'll get the hell outta Dodge."

That's when it slid out from behind the middle column, facing them like a nightmare made real…

TERROR MANNEQUIN!

"Oh, sh-sh-sh—" Weak Bitch stuttered in an unsuccessful attempt to cuss. He pulled back on the swing gate lever with all his weight.

It wouldn't budge.

Just like in the stories, the glowering, sallow, cadaverous-looking mannequin stood holding a grotesquely featured ventriloquist dummy on its left forearm, on whose lap sat a wax doll with a half-melted face, on whose lap sat a crude, faceless voodoo doll. An unopened jack-in-the-box occupied the voodoo doll's lap—the end of one of its blunt little limbs rested on the ball-shaped handle of the box's crank. The mannequin shuffled toward them, stiff legs advancing with short, jerky steps.

"Oh, God…" Weak Bitch said as he pooped his pants. He let go of the jammed lever, slumped over in his seat while Tom Two tightly hugged the cowering, trembling ball that was The Membrane.

"Y-you guys…you go ahead without me!" Weak Bitch said, close to passing out. "Save…yourselves! And whatever you do…don't look at the thing if that voodoo doll starts turning the crank!" He wanted to join them—to swim for it and try to make it to the slide—but he was too damn weak.

Still holding the approaching horror in the spotlight of his flashlight, Weak Bitch shoved Tom Two away with his free arm and clenched his eyes shut. "Jump in the water, fellas!" His voice growing increasingly feeble and faltering, he added, "Climb over the gate and swim for it. Take…the slide…down. Then run…fucking…home."

The thing loomed just several terrible steps away.

Tom Two didn't listen to Weak Bitch. Instead, he closed his eyes, grabbed his pillowcase from the floor, reached in, and pulled out his last three pieces of candy: a Nestle's Nursing Home, a Hershey's Hospice, and a Cadbury Crème-atorium.

In case you're not in the know, Nestle's Nursing Homes and Hershey's Hospices are pretty much the same thing. Basically, they're solid milk chocolate versions of those little red hotels used in the boardgame *Monopoly*. In fact, Nestle's Nursing Homes and Hershey's Hospices are the exact same size and shape as those little hotels. That's because the molds used to make Nestle's Nursing Homes and Hershey's Hospices were originally used to produce the *Monopoly* hotels. In 1983, Nestle and Hershey's acquired them from Hasbro for that express purpose. Or maybe it was 1997. Or maybe it was 2006. Or maybe it was 1812, the year of that lame war nobody remembers anything about. I actually don't remember what year Nestle and Hershey's acquired the hotel molds, but it probably doesn't matter. Who fucking cares? I mean, Google it if you want. Anyhow, as for Cadbury Crème-atoriums, they are identical to Nestle's Nursing Homes and Hershey's Hospices save for the fact that they have taller chimneys.

    His eyes still closed, Tom Two held out the three wrapped pieces of chocolate in his trembling hands, the sides of his palms pressed together to form a bowl. The jack-in-the-box began playing "Pop Goes the Weasel."

    As the jingly melody plinked its way to the inevitable "Pop!" Weak Bitch and Tom Two braced themselves, turned their faces away, and clenched their eyelids shut while The Membrane wrapped itself into an even tighter ball.

    At the moment when the "Pop!" note played, they heard a somewhat anticlimactic click, presumably the sound of the box's lid flipping open, followed by silence.

    "Don't...don't look!" Weak Bitch repeated in a near whisper.

    But unable to resist his curiosity, and against his better judgement, Tom Two opened one of his eyes, creating a narrow slit. He thought a little peek wouldn't do any harm.

Suspended at the end of a black spring jutting out of the open box was a small, golden brown lump.

It was a Chicken McNugget.

With a goddamn face!

The lines of this little visage—mouth pulled in an uneven frown, brow furrowed in an angry-looking "v" above pinpoint eyes—glowed orange-red as if from a candle burning within the thing's diminutive, battered, deep-fried form. It wore a multicolored, three-pointed jester cap with a tiny bell at the end of each dangling sleeve. As Tom Two spied on the thing through his slitted eye, he didn't think it was a super terrifying thing that could kill people by just looking at them like the legend said. On the contrary: though the head was weirdly creepy, Tom Two's overall impression of the thing was that it was *FUCKING STUPID!!*

Tom Two was also pretty damn sure his heart had not just stopped beating and had not turned into a Totino's pizza roll, and he was also certain his brain had not transformed into dogshit at the sight of the thing. Still, as he didn't know what he was dealing with, he decided to err on the side of caution by not letting the thing know he had seen it.

The Chicken McNugget head glanced from the sugary offering in Tom Two's hands to Tom Two's spooky face and back to the candy. It tilted to the side as if puzzled and unsure of how to proceed. The face turned to Weak Bitch, then to The Membrane before returning its fiery-orange gaze to the proffered sweets. Its tiny jaw widening to two times its size in order to accommodate the candy, it dipped down into Tom Two's hands and took one of the chocolates in its mouth—the Hershey's Hospice—before retracting to its original position. After the Chicken McNugget swallowed the Hershey's Hospice, wrapper and all, a lump formed at the top of the spring, which apparently doubled as the thing's neck. The lump descended the spiral and disappeared into the box a moment later.

The creature belched loudly.

"Awwwwwwwwwwwwwwww yeah!" it said, uttering the two words just like a rapper would, though its voice was inhumanly deep and gritty.

That's when Weak Bitch passed out from blood loss, his hand releasing the flashlight and letting it fall to the floor of the boat with a hollow clunk.

Chapter 17

Despite his blurry vision, when Weak Bitch opened his eyes after regaining consciousness, he found himself staring up into the harrowing faces of the Chicken McNugget-in-a-box and the wax doll. He screamed, thrust his arms out. The doll, which grasped a sewing needle in one little fist and a length of suturing thread in the other, pulled away to dodge his flailing arms, as did the Chicken McNugget head.

"Everything's okay, my friend," a man's resonant baritone voice said. "They're just stitching up your lip, is all. We're taking care of you, bro." The voice was warm, kind, and comforting. As a matter of fact, Weak Bitch thought it might be the most chill voice he'd ever heard in his life. Then someone grasped his arms and gently pushed them back down to his sides. "Easy now," the mellifluous voice said. "You don't want to rip your IV out of your arm."

That's when Weak Bitch realized he was in a bed, the back of his head half-sunk in a soft pillow. He turned his head to the left, toward the sound of the voice, but everything beyond an arm's reach was a blur.

"But...but," Weak Bitch said, struggling to speak.

"Easy now, son," the voice said. "You need to rest. We'll talk later."

"But...but...I...just...saw...fucking...TERROR MANNEQUIN."

"That wasn't TERROR MANNEQUIN," the chill voice said. Then the voice faded away along with the rest of the world as Weak Bitch sank back into unconsciousness.

***

His vision was much clearer when he regained consciousness again a bit later, and the pain in his eyes and lower lip had dulled to a tolerable soreness. He felt mellow, warm, lightheaded, and unworried—as if he were mildly medicated. Looking around, he observed he was in what appeared to be a sparsely furnished, windowless bedroom. Tom Two and The Membrane were seated in chairs off to the left against the wall. A big glass bowl of candy rested in Tom Two's lap from which he and The Membrane ate greedily. Standing beside his nephews was the thing that had stitched up his lip: the hybrid mannequin/ventriloquist dummy/wax doll/voodoo doll/jack-in-the-box abomination that looked like the legendary TERROR MANNEQUIN, but was *not* TERROR MANNEQUIN according to what the soothing voice had said.

Beside the monster stood a scrawny, sixtyish man attired in a Bob Ross "Happy Little Trees" t-shirt, a pair of faded blue jeans, and an old beat-up pair of Timbs. His long, thin hair was mostly gray, though streaked with dishwater blond and pulled back in a tight ponytail. He wore an equally long beard, which was twined into two Viking braids. A pair of retro round sunglasses with red-orange lenses hid the man's eyes.

"Holy shit!" Weak Bitch said, recognizing him. "Could it really be? Are you…Chillington, the Chillmaster of Chillville?"

"I am," Chillington, the Chillmaster of Chillville, said in the most chill voice imaginable.

Chillville was a village in southern Ohio that was known worldwide as being, in all likelihood, the most chill city on Earth. Citizens of Chillville only worked two months out of the year, rotating shifts in the village's world-famous brewery and on the lush marijuana farms that encircled Chillville's small, quaint downtown area. During their ample downtime, the villagers—known as a chillagers—just basically hung out, enjoying a life of rest, relaxation, and recreation.

Until recently, the title of Chillville's highest elected official had been Chillmaster. More like spiritual leaders than actual governing officials, Chillmasters had served lifelong terms, but could be impeached if they were ever observed to engage in unchill (i.e., asshole-ish) behavior, which almost never happened. When a Chillmaster died, the chillagers held a vote to decide who was the new chillest person in town, and that person became the next Chillmaster.

Chillington had been Chillmaster of Chillville for the last forty years. But in 1989, he left town to go on sabbatical at an undisclosed location outside the country, promising to return in a month's time. Only he never came back. To this day, he was presumed dead, but Chillington was so beloved by the chillagers of Chillville that his successor took the title of "Chillminister" so that Chillington would always be remembered as the last Chillmaster of Chillville.

"But aren't you, like, dead?" Weak Bitch asked.

"He who is truly chill never really dies," Chillington said. The man was known for uttering sage aphorisms like this one, usually about the nature of chillness. "No, I'm not dead. I've only been in hiding. And I was doing a pretty good job of staying hidden until you, on the brink of death, floated into my house tonight with your friends. Now, it wouldn't have been very chill of me to just let you bleed to death in that canoe, would it have?"

"Um, no, I guess not. Thanks for saving my life."

Chillington bowed his head slightly in acknowledgement.

Weak Bitch touched his lower lip, ran his finger over the stitches. He glanced down at the IV catheter in his arm. A tube led from the catheter to a bag of translucent purple fluid hanging from a metal pole beside the bed.

"Hey, what's the purple stuff you're giving me?"

"What, did you think Chillington, the Chillmaster of Chillville, would give you a regular old, boring saline drip? Nah, man. You get the good stuff around here. That solution is infused with some of the best purple chronic from Chillville's world-famous cannabis farms."

"Whoa. Well, that explains this wicked mellow feeling I have—I'm fuckin' high as a kite." Weak Bitch pushed himself up in bed, rolled his shoulders, and twisted his head around to stretch his stiff neck. "How long have I been out for?"

"About an hour."

"Shit. Seems longer." Weak Bitch glanced down at his legs. "Hey, why am I wearing sweatpants? Where are my jeans?"

"The sweatpants are a loaner from me. Don't you remember? You, um, fouled yourself in the canoe."

Tom Two and The Membrane shook with silent laughter in their chairs. The Membrane formed its limbs and signed a message: *Haha, you pooped your pants like a big baby!*

Weak Bitch cast The Membrane a dirty look, then the candy bowl caught his attention. "Oh, shit. Hey, you shouldn't have given them candy. It's illegal to give Tom Two and The Membrane candy on Halloween."

"But you came here tonight to trick-or-treat. You're the first trick-or-treaters I've ever had out here actually."

"We didn't come here to trick-or-treat. We came here to *reverse* trick-or-treat."

Chillington frowned. "And what, might I ask, is reverse trick-or-treating?"

"I'll tell you," Weak Bitch said, "but first I have some questions of my own." He pointed at the mannequin. "For starters, if that thing is *not* TERROR MANNEQUIN, then what the hell is it?"

"Oh, that's just Aw-Yeah. He's basically my personal servant, bodyguard, and personal chef all rolled into one. He may look like TERROR MANNEQUIN, but trust me: Aw-Yeah is chill as hell."

"Why is he called Aw-Yeah?" Weak Bitch asked.

"Because he can only speak one phrase. Anyway, how about we continue our conversation in the living room? I'll have Aw-Yeah fetch us some refreshments."

As if on cue, the Chicken McNugget's mouth hole widened to say, "Awwwwwwwwwwww yeah!"

Chapter 18

Sundry Halloween lights and decorations—such as orange and black lava lamps and skull-shaped plasma balls flickering with green and purple electricity—adorned Fallingwater's spacious living room. Heavy black drapes cloaked the windows in the room, preventing even a pinpoint of light from shining through to the world outside. An immense C-shaped sofa dominated the space, where Chillington bade Weak Bitch, Tom Two, and The Membrane to kick back and make themselves comfortable.

Chill instrumental music played at a low volume from unseen, super-high-end speakers throughout the room. The music's hypnotic, slow-funk drum groove lent it a kind of smooth jazz feel while the ambient synth and slightly dissonant, reverb-washed guitar comping above the groove added an ethereal, almost otherworldly quality to the music. Weak Bitch and Tom Two both found themselves bobbing their heads to the music while The Membrane's entire form twitched in time with the beat.

"Man, what's this music you're playing?" Weak Bitch asked. "It's chill as hell."

"It's called chillcore. Glad you like it. It's a music genre I invented myself. I recorded this album in my home studio here at Fallingwater."

Weak Bitch and his nephews sat across from their host, who packed a tall octopus-shaped hookah with purple chronic, fired that mofo up, and took a deep pull off a hose. Holding the smoke in his chest, he proffered the hose to Weak Bitch.

"No thanks. I think I'm high enough as it is, my tiny little weak bitch."

Chillington's head jerked up as he coughed, expelling a long plume of purple smoke. "Did you just call me your tiny little weak bitch?"

Weak Bitch chuckled. "Oops. Yeah, I did. Sorry. Not sure why I said that. I guess I'm just really high. Heh. See, *my* name is My Tiny Little Weak Bitch."

"Surely you can't be serious about that, compadre."

"Unfortunately, I am, man. My boss made me legally change my name to My Tiny Little Weak Bitch yesterday. It was either that or get canned."

"Whoa. That's not chill at all."

"Yeah, tell me about it."

"Well, I'm not about to call you My Tiny Little Weak Bitch. What was your name before that?"

"Glont Lamont."

"Then I'm calling you Glont." (Dear Reader: Since Chillington, the Chillmaster of Chillville, insists on calling him Glont, let us go back to doing the same.)

Aw-Yeah returned from the kitchen, the dummy part of it bearing a large silver tray that contained jack-o-lantern-shaped sugar cookies, bat-shaped brownies, caramel apples, apple cider, and a metal bucket filled with chilly bottles of Chillington Brewery's own Chilltoberfest dark lager (8.7 percent alcohol by volume).

"Would you all like a beer?" Chillington asked, to which The Membrane immediately gave an enthusiastic thumbs up.

"Me and The Membrane will. Thanks," Glont said. "But apple cider for Tom Two. He's not old enough to drink alcohol."

"Not old enough, eh?" Chillington said. "How old are you, Tom Two?"

Tom Two signed at him: *Eons old.*

"Luckily I'm adept at sign language," Chillington said. "For, as I've always said, 'He who masters sign language is chill as hell.' So you're likely *eons old*, you say?" Chillington turned to Glont, one eyebrow arched in confusion.

"*Might* be eons old," Glont said, "But he's also two years old. I know, that doesn't really make a lick of sense. It's kind of hard to explain."

"Well, then explain away, my friend. I'm all ears. I've never had visitors here before. All these things you see here—the good food, the abundant herb, the ever-flowing brew, this chill house itself—well, I haven't been able to share them with anyone. Hence, I'm delighted to have your company and would love to hear your dudes' stories. So how about you tell me about you, then I'll tell you about me, okay? But first, I just have to ask, why were you reverse trick-or-treating here tonight? I mean, no one ever comes out here. Did you not see all my NO TRESPASSING signs?"

Tom Two hopped to his feet on the couch, arms and hands signing with much animation to inform Chillington that they would never have come if Chillington hadn't removed the barbed wire fence and the NO TRESPASSING signs around the property.

"I didn't remove my barbed wire fence or those signs!"

Well, someone sure did, Chillingsworth, The Membrane signed.

It's "Chillington," not "Chillingsworth," Tom Two signed to correct him.

"Damn, I should've known," Glont said. "It was someone from town. I bet whoever it was did it so we'd have to come out here tonight. They probably hoped we'd run into TERROR MANNEQUIN and get killed."

I bet Lance Montgomery was in on it, Tom Two signed.

"Nah, I don't think so. If Lance had wanted us to come out here tonight, he wouldn't have tried to make me kill myself earlier. It could have been just about anyone else in town though since everyone loathes you guys. I guess it really doesn't matter who did it. Fuck 'em all."

Yeah, yo, fuck this whole flaming-turd town in the ass with a big, blue, sweet, spiked dick, mang! The Membrane signed.

***

Glont told Chillington all about Tom Two and The Membrane: about their enigmatic, apparently supernatural natures, their strange and unexplained origins, their connection to the Lamont ancestral home, their ostracization and persecution by the hard-hearted residents of Selohssa, and the cruel tradition of reverse trick-or-treat. He also told Chillington about himself; about his role as a caregiver for his nephews and ailing mother; about how, despite having the perfect job, he hated it; about how he longed to work grueling, demoralizing, soul-crushing, 15-hour shifts seven-days-a-week as a coal miner or maybe a sewer cleaner or perhaps a roadkill scraper-upper; and about how he hadn't gotten his dick wet in something like twenty years, not since the last time he'd had blindfolded sex with Ma-He's-Makin'-Eyes-At-Me.

Chillington listened to it all intently, his face screwed into an intense, focused expression as he took in and contemplated all the sundry injustices with which Glont regaled him. When Weak finished telling their stories, Chillington exhaled a spiraling ribbon of purple smoke and said, "Man, I'm really sorry to hear about that dry dick of yours, but I'm even more sorry to hear you don't dig working for my company anymore. I mean, I understand though. The super-chill, super-idle life isn't for everyone."

Glont went wide-eyed. "*Your* company?"

"Yeah. I'm, like, Fun 4-Life's anonymous founder, majority shareholder, and its secret CEO."

"No way," Glont said, incredulous.

"Kinda crazy, huh?"

"So is that why you've holed yourself up here at Fallingwater all these years? To be closer to your company?"

"Oh, no. I haven't had much to do with Fun 4-Life since even before my disappearance from Chillville, at least not directly. That company always just sorta took care of itself. It's mostly funded by profits from Chillville's brewery and marijuana farms, but I've been more or less high and/or blackout drunk for the last thirty years, so I honestly can't remember the last time I checked in to see what was going on with Fun 4-Life or any of my many other assets and investments for that matter. But from what you're tellin' me, hoss, it looks like some very unchill motherfuckers have infiltrated senior and middle management over there."

"Well, they're not all bad. I mean, Marty—my floor manager—is kinda a dick, but he's alright most of the time, I guess, despite dressing up like a big baby every day and forcing employees to change his poopy diapers. But Lance Montgomery? Yeah, that guy's the fucking worst. Shit, he's the one who nearly killed me tonight!"

Glont cracked open another Chilltoberfest as Chillington continued to sit quietly across from him, a contemplative look on his face.

"So if you didn't come out here to be close to your company…" Glont started to ask, but caught his tongue, thinking he was being too nosey.

"Then why did I come out here?" Chillington finished for him. "You want to know what would possess me to abandon the most chill city on the planet to come out here and live like a hermit for three decades and counting?"

"Yeah," Glont said as Tom Two and The Membrane both signed a *yes*.

"Well, the short answer is that thirty years ago, I, Chillington, the Chillmaster of Chillville—and although I am deeply ashamed to admit it—began to have certain unkind—nay, certain *unchill*—thoughts."

Suddenly wide-eyed, Tom Two gasped and raised both his hands to his mouth in shock.

Chapter 19

Chillington explained that, as the most chill people on Earth, the chillagers of Chillville had always adhered to a strict policy of Gandhi- and Thoreau-inspired pacifism. In their code of chill behavior, violence was considered very unchill, so all chillagers were taught from a very young age to turn the other cheek and to resolve conflicts via nonviolent means, at least whenever possible.

"But around thirty years ago," he said, "whenever I was made aware of the innumerable assholes populating the world outside of Chillville—be it assholes I encountered while travelling on business, those I saw on TV, or those I heard on the radio—I began to feel a mounting anger like I'd never felt before, anger that eventually ballooned into a rage. This rage, in turn, gave birth to bad—nay, violent—thoughts. Sick violent fantasies—fantasies of me beating and tearing unchill people apart with my bare hands. And with these fantasies came feelings of great shame, shame at ever having entertained such unchill thoughts. As a result, I began to fear I was no longer fit to be the leader of Chillville and its public face. That's when I decided to go away on a retreat. I wanted to go someplace quiet and isolated, a place where I could purge my head of unchill thoughts and recharge spiritually. So I called my old friend, the retired oil tycoon Silas Amadeus Cruthers XVII, and asked him if I could come stay at Fallingwater for a few weeks."

Glont nearly choked on his beer. "You were friends with Silas Amadeus Cruthers XVII?"

"Yes. Silas and I went way back. In fact, I had been something of a spiritual adviser to him during the final years of his life. The man regarded me as one of his only friends. I'd been a guest here many times before my sabbatical, so Silas was more than willing to accommodate me by giving me private access to the house's recently and secretly constructed basement, which the Old Man had used for top secret business meetings prior to his retirement. To avoid any unwanted visits from the paparazzi, he promised to keep my stay here a secret from the rest of the world, including from his own house servants and security guards.

"When I first arrived here for my retreat, I spent a lot of time practicing tai chi, kung fu, yoga, and Zen meditation. I stayed away from the TV and the radio. I read chill books, including a number of ancient chill texts, smoked a lot of chill weed, and exercised a lot. The basement here connects to a tunnel that leads to a secret door in the ravine not too far downstream from the swimming hole at the end of the water slide. That passage allowed me to come and go as I pleased without worrying that anyone in the house would see me. As such, I spent a lot of my time here going for walks in the woods, communing with nature.

"But after a month, I found myself still unable to exorcise the violent thoughts from my head. The retreat just wasn't having its desired effect. I realized I needed a more effective method to rid myself of unchill thoughts, and I just so happened to stumble upon such a method in a book on Treetrap-Foofap-Glargarianism that I'd brought with me to Fallingwater."

"Treetrap...*what?*" Glont asked.

"Treetrap-Foofap-Glargarianism. It's a type of folk spirituality—essentially a hybrid of Tibetan Buddhist mysticism, Haitian voodoo, and Eastern Siberian shamanism. The Treetrap-Foofap-Glargarianism text I read spoke of something called tulpas, a concept originating in Tibetan Buddhist mysticism. Tulpas are sentient, willful beings created by concentrated thought. The text spoke of different types of tulpas and the proper mental techniques by which to create them. Of particular interest to me was a type of tulpa known as a slee-slaw. A slee-slaw is a physical manifestation of its maker's own concentrated bad thoughts. They are created when a person wants to permanently rid themselves of such thoughts. If the creation of a slee-slaw is successful, the creator must destroy it at the moment of its birth. This way, the maker quite literally destroys his own evil thoughts.

"You can imagine my excitement at my discovery, so I immediately followed the very detailed instructions on how to create a slee-slaw." Chillington paused for a moment, his thin lips pulled into a somber straight line. He turned to the shaded windows, as if staring through them at something out in the woods. "And I...I was successful."

The Membrane signed at Chillington: *So what all is involved with creating a slee-slaw, Chillonardo da Vinci?*

It's "Chillington," not "Chillonardo da Vinci," Tom Two signed to correct him.

"What's involved with creating a slee-slaw?" Chillington said. "Man, you don't even wanna know! Let's just skip over that part."

But I do wanna know, The Membrane signed.

"Why do you wanna know?" Chillington asked.

Man, you don't even wanna know why I wanna know! The Membrane signed.

"Not true. I do wanna know why you wanna know," Chillington said.

Why do you wanna know why I wanna know? The Membrane signed.

"Man, you don't even wanna know why I wanna know why you wanna know!" Chillington said.

On the contrary, Chillexander the Great. I do wanna know why you wanna know why I wanna know, The Membrane signed.

"But why do you wanna know why you wanna know why I wanna know?" Chillington asked.

Believe me, Baron von Chillster. You don't even wanna know why I wanna know why you wanna know why I wanna know! The Membrane signed.

This went on for a long time. In fact, it went on for decades and decades until everyone in this book fucking died and turned into dry white dogshit.

THE END.

Just kidding.

Eventually, Chillington said, "Alright, alright. I'll tell you guys how to make a slee-slaw. It's complicated though. The first thing you have to do is visit a cemetery where a serial killer is buried, dig up the serial killer's grave, dump the corpse, and steal the coffin. Then, after you bring the coffin to someplace private, you fill it with a bunch of items before reburying it exactly three nights before Halloween."

What sort of items, Chillmaster? Tom Two signed.

"Well, first off, and most importantly, you have to put a heavy iron chain with a padlock in there. It will bind and immobilize the slee-slaw after it's born so that you can swiftly destroy it before it ever has a chance to escape the coffin. As far as the other stuff goes, the list is really long, so I probably couldn't tell you everything. But off the top of my head? Let's see: a snippet of sage, a pinch of hemlock, a smidgeon of nightshade, a dash of mandrake root, a splash of rosewater. Oh, you also need some eye of newt, leg of lizard, tail of puppy, face of frog, wing of wasp, brain of bat, boner of bee, and swingin' blue, low-slung nutsack of cockroach. Hm, what else? Oh, a Ouija board dipped in pig's blood. Some of your own clothing, hair, nail clippings, vomit, and feces. You also need six evil dolls obtained from six haunted houses. Three malevolent marionettes. A fetal polar bear cub pickled in a jar of homemade clown tear-infused moonshine. A chimpanzee's head, freshly severed and boiled in wolf piss. Hm, what else? Oh, sixty-nine Blockbuster video cards belonging to sixty-nine different people. And a photograph of Antoni Salieri (the Italian composer and conductor known primarily in modern times as the rumored rival of Wolfgang Amadeus Mozart, at least as he was depicted and popularized in the 1984 film *Amadeus*), but one that happens to be autographed by the lead singer of Soul Asylum."

"Wow," Glont said. "You really got the lead singer of Soul Asylum to autograph a picture of Salieri for you?"

"Yes. I had to. But that was actually relatively easy to acquire compared to some of the other stuff on the list. Like, for example, a live adult great white shark."

"What the?" Glont said. "How the hell did you get a live adult great white shark and get it to fit inside a coffin with all that other stuff?"

"Well, luckily the spell stipulates that if you don't have access to an adult great white shark and/or the mechanical means to stuff and compress an adult great white shark into a space as small as an already crowded coffin, then it's okay to substitute a goldfish for the shark. Anyhow, lastly, you have to add some of your own blood, urine, and semen to the mix, along with a few more bee boners, I think. Then you shut the lid and bury the coffin six feet deep. When you return three nights later on Halloween night, you must stand above the grave and chant the word "slee-slaw" 69 times before you dig up the coffin. If you followed the instructions correctly, when you open the lid, you'll gaze upon your chained up slee-slaw as it struggles in vain to free itself. In this way, the coffin is as much a tomb for the thing as it is a womb.

"Every slee-slaw has a unique appearance, one that usually reflects the fears of its maker. The form mine took reflected my own greatest childhood fears. Namely mannequins, ventriloquist dummies, evil dolls, voodoo dolls, and jack-in-the-boxes.

"Anyway, before a newly birthed, chained-bound slee-slaw gets a chance to escape its coffin, its creator must use a weapon—an ax or a sledge hammer is recommended—to smash its head without delay, thereby dispatching the evil thing and all the bad thoughts it embodies for good. Then, the coffin can be sealed and reburied. Unfortunately, despite my best efforts to follow all the instructions to the letter, I sorta forgot to put one of the required items in the coffin. A very, er, important item."

The Chain! The Membrane signed.

His lips pursed in a grimace, Chillington shook his head in frustration and self-reproach. "Yeah, the friggin' chain, man! And if there's a lesson to be learned here, my chillbros, it is this: if you ever find you need to employ some fucked-up, crazy voodoo shit to create an evil, sentient manifestation of your own homicidal thoughts, don't do it when you're high as a mofo!

"Anyhow, on Halloween night in 1989, just as I was stooping down in that grave to open the coffin to destroy my slee-slaw, the coffin lid flew off, whacked me in the forehead, sent me flying into the dirt wall behind me. The moment before I lost consciousness and crumpled to my knees, I saw the terrible thing stand up in the coffin. When I came to about an hour later, I was lying on my side in the otherwise-empty grave. The slee-slaw was gone. I climbed out to the sight of flashing red and blue emergency lights in the woods back in the direction of Fallingwater. I knew then that I was too late: something terrible had already happened.

"I stole back to the house via the secret passage, where I consulted my book forthwith and learned that a slee-slaw's creator must immediately make another type of tulpa if their slee-slaw escapes them—a sort of counter slee-slaw called a cree-craw. Whereas a slee-slaw is a materialization of bad thoughts, a cree-craw is a manifestation of chill thoughts. When done correctly, the very act of creating a cree-craw automatically destroys the analogous slee-slaw mere moments later, even if the evil thing has fled to the other side of the world. The two beings just sort of cancel each other out like matter and antimatter, both withering away within seconds.

"Wow," Glont said. "So did you have to gather a bunch of weird crap together and bury it in a coffin again?"

"No. The creation of a cree-craw is considerably less complicated than that of a slee-slaw. To create a cree-craw, you just have to light a candle in an otherwise darkened bathroom, flush a couple bee boners down the toilet, and recite the word "cree-craw" sixty-nine times while staring into the mirror, at which point your cree-craw will climb out of it. A cree-craw physically resembles the slee-slaw that it was summoned to counter, but only as a chill parody. Hence, although Aw-Yeah's physical form is similar to TERROR MANNEQUIN's, his jack-in-the-box contains a harmless, rather unterrifying Chicken McNugget on a spring, whereas TERROR MANNEQUIN's jack-in-the-box holds some sort of great evil that kills anyone who looks at it. And while the mannequin part of TERROR MANNEQUIN is the intelligence that controls the smaller parts, with Aw-Yeah, the Chicken McNugget is the brain."

Aw-Yeah's Chicken McNugget rocked up and down in agreement.

"But again, the biggest difference," Chillington said, "is that while TERROR MANNEQUIN is unchill, Aw-Yeah is chill as hell."

Glont asked, "But if the chill cree-craw and the evil slee-slaw were supposed to cancel each other out, then how come Aw-Yeah is still around?"

"Well, I screwed up again. When I was reciting the word 'cree-craw' while looking in the bathroom mirror, I lost count of how many times I'd said it. I think maybe I only said it sixty-eight times. Or maybe seventy-two. What can I say? I fucked it up. Apparently, I suck a big, fat, sweet, spiked blue dick when it comes to black magic and incantations and shit like that. I'm a Chillmaster, my dudes. That sort of thing is just not in my wheelhouse. Anyhow, I inherited Fallingwater after Old Man Cruthers' death."

"No friggin' way!" Glont said. "*You're* the unknown beneficiary of Old Man Cruthers' estate?"

"I am. But I never intended to move here permanently. However, in the aftermath of the tragedy, I just couldn't stand the guilt. See, all those children who fell to their deaths—they died because of *me*—because of *my* errors. So I holed myself up here and had the barbed wire fence put in and all those NO TRESPASSING signs put up. I began to drink and smoke weed more or less all day long to keep the terrible guilt at bay. That's what I've been doing here for the last thirty years. It's only been in the last few weeks that I finally began to sober up a little. During all this time, Aw-Yeah has cooked, cleaned, and run errands for me. To protect my privacy, I also have Aw-Yeah sit in front of the windows and creep around in the woods from time to time so that some trespassers get the occasional glimpse of what they assume is TERROR MANNEQUIN, sending them running away in terror. This helps keep the legend of TERROR MANNEQUIN alive, which helps keep the number of trespassers around here in check."

So was the real TERROR MANNEQUIN destroyed? The Membrane signed.

"Of that, I am virtually certain. It's been thirty years since I made Aw-Yeah, and not once have I come across any evidence that TERROR MANNEQUIN still exists on the grounds of Fallingwater or anywhere else in the world."

Perhaps to express his approval of the Chillmaster's incredible story, Aw-Yeah was all, "Awwwwwwwwwww yeah!"

Chapter 20

"Well, hey, man," Glont said, now fairly buzzed. "I'm glad you're starting to put all that negative shit behind you and sobering up after all this time, healing and whatnot. So are you planning to go back to Chillville?"

Chillington sighed. "I'd love to go back."

"That's great. Shit, those folks are gonna freak when they see you. It'll be a joyous occasion. Probably a big media event, too, I'd think." Glont held his beer up. "Here's to the triumphant, imminent return and joyous homecoming of Chillington, the motherfuckin' goddamn Chillmaster of Chillville!"

The Membrane raised its beer and Tom Two his apple cider, and the three toasted their host.

"Thank you, my friends. But although I'd love to go back, I'm afraid that's impossible."

Why? Tom Two signed.

"Because I still have those unchill thoughts."

"The same ones?" Glont asked. "Like, thoughts about killing people?"

"Yes. And now I realize that the only way I'll ever purge them from my mind is to…to act on them. Well, not literally. I mean, I wouldn't want to actually kill anyone. But if I could just inflict a little pain on some assholes who really deserved it—if I could kick a few asses for once in my life, I think I could rid myself of the unchill thoughts. Like those assholes in town you've been talking about. I'm pretty certain I could free myself of my maddening thoughts if I slapped a few of them around a little, maybe doled out some black eyes and a few busted lips, or a few broken bones at the worst. In fact, I feel it is my destiny to do so. And I believe our destinies are integrally intertwined—that your visit here tonight was not by mere chance."

"But if you physically hurt people, even if they're the biggest fucking assholes on the planet and, like, totally deserve it, won't you have to give up your Chillmaster title?"

"I will. Along with all the privileges that come with it, including the ability to return to my beloved home. In other words, regardless of whether I act on my thoughts or not, I can never go back. So if I must live the rest of my days outside of Chillville, I might as well do so without having to live with the tormenting thoughts."

And teach a few punk-ass suckas a lesson or two in the process! The Membrane signed, undulating with excitement.

Yeah, teach a few punk-ass, whack-ass, uncouth, untoward, uncivil, basic-ass, tiny-dicked motherfuckers a motherfuckin' lesson or two, Tom Two signed, jumping up and down on the sofa.

"Language, Double T!" Glont scolded before turning to Chillington. "Hey, if you're thinking about paying Lance Montgomery a visit, it might not be such a great idea. He and his meathead buddies would kick our drunk, stoned asses."

"Not Aw-Yeah's ass. Remember, Aw-Yeah wasn't even supposed to survive for more than a few minutes beyond his birth. But because I screwed up the cree-craw incantation that brought him here, not only did he survive, but as an unexpected side effect, he possesses superhuman strength. He's kinda like Jason Vorhees or Michael Myers. He also has insane telekinetic powers that render him nearly invincible. Believe me, my chillbros—with Aw-Yeah on our side, no one's kickin' *our* asses.

"So whaddaya say, guys? I think we have a party to crash, huh? But the night is young. It's only twelve fifteen. Can you think of any other mean assholes in town that deserve a little surprise visit from my boy, Aw-motherfucking-Yeah?"

Glont smiled, glancing from Chillington to Tom Two to The Membrane to Aw-Yeah, then back to Chillington. "Well, yeah, that basically describes the whole damned town. But, sure, I can definitely think of a few to start with."

But what if some of them are sorry for being mean to us? Tom Two signed. *What if some of them promise to be kind people from now on?*

"Pfft," Glont said. "I wouldn't hold your breath, Tom Two."

"But he brings up a good point," Chillington said. "It would be unchill of us if we didn't at least offer people a chance to apologize and atone for their past behavior. And who knows? Maybe merely presenting assholes with the threat of physical punishment will be sufficient to purge me of my unchill thoughts."

And then Aw-Yeah was all, "Awwwwwwwwwww yeah!"

Chapter 21

Across the street from the Lamont house, Mr. and Mrs. Brown were reading in bed and just minutes away from turning off their bedside light for the night—Mr. Brown reading *Fuck Everybody Except You: Brutally Cutthroat Tactics to Becoming a Successful Entrepreneur in Late-Capitalist America* while Mrs. Brown was reading *Fifty Shades* for the umpteenth time—when their doorbell rang at 12:30 AM.

Mrs. Brown's hardcover dropped from her face. She turned to her husband, fear in her eyes.

"Damn kids," Mr. Brown said. "It's a little late for ding dong ditch though."

The doorbell rang again several seconds later.

"Damn it!" Mr. Brown said as he slammed his book on the bed and swung his legs out over the floor. In his pajamas, he stomped out of the bedroom and into the hall, where he flicked on the hall light. Mrs. Brown got out of bed and followed him in her nightgown.

When he reached the front vestibule, he turned the porch light on and looked through the peephole. That Glont Lamont asshole from across the street was outside on the front walk with his two freak nephews and some older, long-haired man wearing red-orange sunglasses.

"What the hell?" he grumbled as he turned the deadbolt and released the door chain. He opened the door a crack, his wife peeking over his shoulder. "It's 12:30 in the morning, you morons! You already stopped here for reverse trick-or-treat. Don't ya remember?"

"Hello, friend," Chillington said, taking a step forward, his hands folded at his midriff.

"I'm not *your* friend, pal. Who the fuck are you?"

"I am Chillington, the Chillmaster of Chillville. I've come here tonight to help right a wrong. And if it is possible for me to do so without violence, then I will. For he who is truly chill always pursues the most peaceful resolution first."

"What the hell are you talking about?"

"I'm offering you and your wife a chance to make amends for the years of cruel treatment you've shown my friends here—your neighbors from across the street. All you have to do is apologize to them, right here and now, and promise to treat them with common courtesy and neighborly goodwill from here on out."

"Pfft!" Mr. Brown spat before letting out a sardonic chuckle. He pushed the door open wider, leaned out into the night. "Hey, I got better idea, you dirty hippy. How about you all turn your ugly, freak asses around and march the hell off my property before I call the fucking cops, eh?"

Mr. Brown was about to slam the door shut when Aw-Yeah stepped out from behind a tree on the front lawn and approached the house with the ventriloquist dummy's free hand held out before it, reaching for the Browns. The moment Mr. and Mrs. Brown saw the thing, they both froze in place in the doorway, paralyzed, eyes bulging with horror.

"Bring them out onto the stoop," Chillington said.

The dummy folded its wooden fingers into its palm, beckoning the Browns forward, who waddled stiffly out from their front doorway, husband followed by wife, both no longer in control of their bodies. They halted at the middle of the stoop, frozen and silent in terror.

"Now what?" Glont asked as he stood on the grass behind Chillington and Aw-Yeah.

"Now it's payback time," Chillington said. He turned to Tom Two and The Membrane. "This is personal for you two. If either of you would like to go first, be my guest."

Tom Two glanced from the frozen, silent, terror-stricken Browns to Chillington, a confused look on his face. *Go first?* he signed. *Go first at what?*

"At teaching these folks a lesson, my tiny little chilltastic son."

What should I do to them? Tom Two signed.

"Do whatever you want. Maybe start off with a punch to the stomach? Perhaps a stomp to the foot."

Tom Two turned to Glont, the look in his eyes asking his uncle if all of this was okay.

"Go ahead," Glont said, though halfheartedly. "I mean, that's why we came back here."

Tom Two shrugged his shoulders. He took a hesitant step forward, climbed the steps to the stoop. As the idea of inflicting physical harm on anyone was completely foreign to him, he stepped on Mr. Brown's feet, one at a time, but with barely enough force for him to feel anything. Next, he lightly slapped one of Mrs. Brown's hands, though it was more like a pat.

Nevertheless, he pointed up at her face and signed, *That's for all the times you said you would slap my little hand!* He marched back down the steps to the others, proud he had finally gotten sweet, sick, brutal revenge on those two fuckers.

"That's all you want to do to them, Tom Two?" the Chillmaster asked.

Tom Two nodded.

"Suit yourself," Chillington said before addressing The Membrane. "How about you, my slithery, slimy friend? You wanna go next?"

The Membrane formed a limb, used it to grab a stick off the lawn, and slid up the steps to the Browns. Like Tom Two, the thing was unaccustomed to hurting people. It smarted Mr. Brown's knee with the stick and whacked Mrs. Brown across the ass, barely causing either one much discomfort, before it slid back down the steps.

"Glont, my dude," Chillington said. "How about you? You want to get in on the action?"

"Eh, I think I'll pass. Hey, ya know what? Maybe we've gone far enough. I mean, look at them. They're, like, scared shitless from being supernaturally paralyzed. I don't think they'll be disrespecting Tom Two or The Membrane again anytime soon, not with the possibility of Aw-Yeah ever coming back here to pay them another visit."

"That may very well be true," Chillington said, "but I'd like to take a turn, too, before we leave." He paused, regarding the Browns as he stroked his beard contemplatively with one hand. "Hey, guys," he said, turning to his companions. "Why didn't the skeleton dance at the Halloween party?"

Glont did a quick shoulder shrug, thinking it an odd time to crack jokes. The Membrane sprouted two temporary shoulders and did the same thing.

Tom Two, however, signed a response: *Because he had no body to dance with.*

Chillington clapped his hands together loudly. "Ha! Tom Two wins the prize." The Chillmaster gestured at the Browns, still frozen on their front stoop like statues. "Hey, speaking of dancing skeletons: Aw-Yeah, yank these assholes' skeletons out of their bodies and make them dance, but keep their brains and eyes intact inside their skulls so they stay alive for a few moments—so that their skeleton dance is the last fucking thing they experience on this mortal plane."

"What the?" Glont mumbled.

"Ready, Aw-Yeah? On one. Five...four...three..."

The dummy clenched its hand into a trembling fist, knuckles facing up, the Chicken McNugget head bobbing up and down in approval.

"...two...ONE!"

On one, the dummy quickly pulled its arm back close to its body, its fist tucking into its side as if in a martial arts stance. At the same time, Mr. and Mrs. Brown's skeletons tore through the flesh, fat, and hides of their bodies to step out into the chilly night. Bloody, wet, and steaming, the backs of their ribcages momentarily opened like swinging doors, leaving their internal organs behind with the rest of their ruptured husks. Their rent, limp, boneless bodies remained standing for a split second before collapsing into two piles of gore and shredded nightclothes.

The skeletonized Mr. and Mrs. Brown, their jawbones hanging loosely in silent screams, locked their bony hands and descended the steps while their still-seeing eyes gleamed wetly with something far beyond mere mortal terror. The group parted to let them pass onto the lawn, where Mr. Brown took one of Mrs. Brown' skeletal hands in his own and placed his other hand on the back of her ribcage, at which point the pair launched into a clumsy box step waltz. All the while, the dummy's free hand and fingers waved in the air—a puppet master pulling invisible, telekinetic strings that led to the glistening crimson skeletons.

While Glont, Tom Two, and The Membrane looked on in shock, disgust, and terror, Chillington laughed and clapped to the broken rhythm of the skeletons' dance. "Yeehaw!" he cried. "Hey, make them do-si-do, Aw-Yeah!"

Glont noticed a change in the Chillmaster's voice: his chill baritone pitch had shifted to a higher register, a shrill inflection that made Glont think he was on the verge of a mental breakdown.

The skeletons broke contact, circled around each other, and returned to their original positions. The life started to abandon their horrified eyes as their oxygen-deprived brains continued to rapidly starve to death.

Chillington kept laughing and clapping. "Swing your partner round and round. C'mon, now! That's it. Now do the running man. There ya go! Now, twerk that little tailbone, Mrs. Brown. Atta' girl! Grind that coccyx into your hubby's pelvis! Now spank that, er, nonexistent ass, Mr. Brown. Heh-heh. Okay, okay, that's enough."

The skeletons froze. Mr. Brown's was upright with Mrs. Brown's bent over in front of it, caught mid-twerk as Aw-Yeah's unholy power prevented them from collapsing.

Over by the tree that Aw-Yeah had hidden behind, Chillington picked a thick stick off the ground and approached the skeletons. Gripping the makeshift club with two hands, he cocked back and knocked Mr. Brown's skull off with one hard swing, sending it flying toward the street.

"Homerun out to centerfield!" he said. "Haha!"

He proceeded to beat both skeletons down to a pile of wet red bones on the lawn. When he was finished, he dropped the stick and turned to the others.

"Alright then. So where to next?" he said very casually.

Tom Two stood with his hands covering his eyes while The Membrane quivered in a scrunched-up ball at his side. Glont stood aghast. He lowered the hand he had cupped over his mouth.

"You said you weren't going to kill anyone. You said you were just going to rough them up a bit, bust some lips, and maybe break some bones at the worst, remember?"

Chillington eyed the pile of bloody bones, his face suddenly paling. "Wow. I...I don't know what came over me. Oh, dear. What have I done? I went way too far. I...I'm so sorry. I, too, am absolutely horrified by what just happened."

You didn't seem so horrified two seconds ago, Glont thought.

Chillington inhaled and exhaled deeply, as if smelling the night air for the first time. "But what's done cannot be undone. And it appears to be working: I already feel better. My brain is now slightly less cluttered with unchill thoughts than before we came here. But, yes, unfortunately these murders weren't necessary. I'm now certain I can derive the same benefits by just scaring people and roughing them up a bit. I know I could never ever kill again."

Tom Two removed his hands from his eyes and signed at Chillington: *You promise?*

"I promise, little chillster."

And Aw-Yeah was all, Awwwwwwwwwwwwww yeah!"

Chapter 22

"What in the blue fuck?" a bleary-eyed Russ Robinson, the town's alcoholic dog-catcher, asked as he stood framed in his front doorway. Not fifteen minutes ago, he'd fallen into a fitful, drunken sleep on his recliner while watching TV, then the doorbell had awakened him.

"I am Chillington, the Chillmaster of Chillville. I've come here tonight to help right a wrong. And if it is possible for me to do so without violence, then I shall…"

Russ's bottom lip trembled in mounting anger, eyes bulging, as Chillington explained the reason for their late-night visit. When the Chillmaster finished, Russ said, "You talkin' to me, fucker?"

"I am."

"Listen, turdmaster. Or fagmaster. Or whatever the fuck you said yer name was. No one comes onto *my* property, tells *me* what to do, and then threatens *me*! You and these freaks have about three seconds to get the hell outta here, or I'm-a come out there and knock yer goddamn teeth out, ya dirty hippy!"

Chillington lowered and shook his head in mock disappointment. "I'm sorry you feel that way, sir." He glanced back at Glont, then at Tom Two and The Membrane before regarding Russ again. "Hey, asshole. You ever wonder what it would be like to dance with your own alimentary canal?"

"Now wait a minute," Glont said, taking a step forward. "You promised, man. No more killing. Nothing worse than a few broken bones, remember?"

Ignoring him, Chillington snapped his fingers and called, "Aw-Yeah!" prompting the cree-craw to step out from the dark shrubs that flanked the end of the porch.

"That does it," Russ said as he stepped outside, nearly tripping over the doorsill. He hadn't noticed Aw-Yeah yet. He thrust his fists out before him like a stumblebum boxer. "I'm about to knock you into the middle of next week, fucker."

"Aw-Yeah, make this asshole dance with his alimentary canal."

Before Glont could protest further, Russ doubled over and vomited his entire digestive tract into his arms in less than twenty seconds, his wide-open jaw dislocating with a sickening pop to accommodate the girth of his stomach. After his inside-out anus slipped out of his gaping mouth, Russ straightened his posture, held the drooping, blubbery red mess out before him, and commenced dancing on the porch, coils of intestines falling to the floorboards with a wet thud as he did so.

"C'mon now, boy!" Chillington cried, clapping his hands with insane glee. "Swing your partner round and round! Heh-heh! Faster, ya old drunk! Haha. That's better. Now, do the cabbage patch. Wow, you're white as hell, man! Haha. Now do the moonwalk! Hey, not bad, whitey. Heh. Whoa, you know what? It looks like you have a big-ass tumor growing on your stomach. Might want to get that checked out, hoss. Haha! Alright, alright, that's enough."

Russ's carcass ceased its horrific dance, toppled down the porch steps, and landed near Chillington's feet tangled in its own viscera. Chillington knelt down, inserted his hand into the gore, raised his bloody fingers close to his face, and examined them for a moment in open-mouthed awe before gingerly inserting them into his mouth. He then glanced over his shoulder at the horror-stricken faces of Glont and Tom Two, as if he'd forgotten they were there, his bloody fingertips still in his mouth. He yanked them out as if he'd just been caught red-handed doing something bad, which of course he had—quite literally.

"Oh, dear," Chillington said. He rose to his feet, wiping the blood onto his jacket. "What have I done? I...I'm afraid I went too far again."

"You broke your promise," Glont said.

"I...I did. I'm so sorry."

"Hey, man. Ya know what? This shit's getting a little too fucked up for us. I think it's time for me to take Tom Two and The Membrane home. It's been a long night."

"Please, my friends. Give me another chance. I promise this won't ever happen again. No more killing. From here on out, I'm just gonna have Aw-Yeah make people punch themselves in the face. Black eyes and busted lips. Nothing worse than that."

"I don't know, man. That's two times now you went back on your word." Glont turned to Tom Two. "Whaddaya think, Double T? Should we give him another chance?"

Tom Two nodded and turned to Chillington. *You promise to keep your promise this time?* he signed.

"I promise to keep my promise, Tom Two. Cross my heart and hope to die."

Chapter 23

Wearing pajamas and scowling something fierce, Selohssa Clerk of Courts Laura Higgins opened her front door a crack. She saw Chillington first, then opened the door a little wider when she spotted Glont and the boys hanging a little farther back on her front walk. "My Tiny Little Weak Bitch? What the hell are you doing here?" She regarded Chillington. "And who the hell are you?"

"I am Chillington, the Chillmaster of Chillville. I've come here tonight to help right a wrong. And if it is possible for me to do so without violence, then I shall. For he who is truly chill always pursues—"

"Fuck you, ya old coot. Get the hell outta my yard before I call the cops!"

"It's rude to interrupt people!" Chillington said. "As I was saying, miss, he who is truly chill always pursues the most peaceful resolution first. Tonight, I'm offering you a chance to…"

After Chillington finished his spiel, Laura said, "Treat *them* with common decency? These freaks—these abominations in the sight of both God and nature? Yeah, right. Now, get the fuck outta here, or I'm gonna call the fucking cops!"

"Aw-Yeah!" Chillington said as he snapped his fingers, causing the cree-craw to step out of the shadows into the pool of light that spilled from the wall lantern beside the door. The ventriloquist dummy pointed at the woman, freezing her in the doorway.

Glont stepped up to Chillington's side, tapped him on the shoulder. "Hey, don't forget about your promise."

"I have not forgotten. Aw-Yeah, make her come outside."

Wide-eyed with primitive fear, Laura opened the door, stepped out onto the stoop.

"Make her punch herself in the face," Chillington said. "Repeatedly."

"Not too hard though," Glont said.

"Not too hard," Chillington echoed him perfunctorily.

The woman balled her hands into fists and commenced punching herself in the face, the dummy deftly working those invisible puppet strings with its fingers. After about twenty seconds, her face was puffy and red, and a light trickle of blood had sprung from her busted lower lip.

"Yeah, take that you wicked bitch!" Glont said. "Serves ya right. Ha. Hey, I think she's had enough though."

Arms folded across his chest, eyes still hidden behind his shades, the Chillmaster did not respond. The woman continued to use her own face as a punching bag. Blood started to leak from nose.

"Hey, man!" Glont said. "I said that's enough already!"

Shaking his lowered head in mounting fury, his lips pulling away from his gnashing teeth, Chillington cried, "Aw-Yeah, make this bitch punch herself so hard in the head that it explodes. Like motherfucking *Scanners,* yo!"

"No!" Glont yelled.

But it was too late.

Laura lifted her arms out to her sides while raising her fists into the air, as if she were flexing her biceps. She then lowered her elbows toward her flanks and drove her fists into the sides of her head in a powerful double impact that caused it to explode like motherfucking *Scanners*. Blood, brains, and skull chunks rained down on the group. The woman's bloody-brainy fists rested knuckle to knuckle in the space where her head had just been.

"Look!" Chillington said. "It's like she just gave herself a fist bump! But her big, fat, idiot head got in the way! Hahaha…"

"Jesus, fuck!" Glont yelled while flinging a pinkish-gray gob of brains out of his hair. "Why the hell did you do that? You broke your fucking promise again!"

Chillington plucked a bit of brain out of his beard. Regarding it intently for a moment, he placed it into his mouth and began to slowly chew.

"Dude!" Glont said. He turned away from the Chillmaster, grabbed a stunned, aghast Tom Two by the shoulder, and said, "C'mon, guys. Let's get the hell outta here."

"No! Wait!" Chillington cried, dropping to his knees, wringing his hands in supplication. "Please don't go! I know—I fucked up again. I'm fucking sorry. I promise I won't kill anybody else! Please, just give me one more fucking chance!"

Glont halted, turned around to face him. "Yeah, right. You've said that three times now! At this point, we'd have to be some dumbass motherfuckers to believe anything you say."

"I know, I know. Listen, I've certainly given you no reason to trust me. But this time is different, I swear it! I finally feel like I'm in control of my impulses. I promise—with the next person we visit, it'll only be to give them a good scare!"

"Man, there's no way we're falling for this shit again," Glont said. "So long, Chillington. It was nice meeting you. And thanks again for saving my life. But, yeah, it's time for us to part ways."

"But I really mean it this time! I promise I won't kill anyone else. I swear I won't. Why, I'll swear on the Holy Bible! That's right. Go get me a Bible, and I'll swear on it right now!"

The Membrane suddenly darted back toward the house.

"No, 'Brane!" Glont shouted after it. "We're leaving!"

But The Membrane kept moving, slid up the porch steps and past the clerk of courts's headless corpse before entering the house.

Glont smacked his forehead in frustration.

A moment later, the thing came back out the front door, an old hardback copy of the Revised Standard Version of the Bible riding its back.

"Now, that's the spirit," Chillington said, still on his knees as The Membrane halted before him. The Chillmaster placed his left hand on the Bible, raised his right hand into the air.

He stared at Glont. "I Chillington, the Chillmaster of Chillville, do solemnly swear on this Holy Bible that I won't kill any more people tonight or ever again."

Tom Two tugged on Glont's jacket. Glont looked down at him. Tom Two signed, *Well, he must be telling the truth now since he swore on the Holy Bible!*

"I dunno, Double T. I'm not so certain him swearing on a Bible means he's telling the truth."

"Please, my friend," Chillington said, wringing his hands again. "Just give me one more chance."

For his part, Tom Two fell to his knees and signed, *Yes, please, Uncle Glont! Let's give him one more chance.* The Membrane also joined in, forming two limbs and two crude hands to wring.

"Alright, alright," Glont said, giving in against his better judgement. He jabbed a finger at Chillington. "But this is your last fucking chance, pal. Like, for real!"

Chapter 24

"Can I help you?" Sharon Simmons asked in her open doorway. She was the woman whose son had dressed up as Chucky and tried to hit Tom Two in the knee with a stick earlier that night.

"Yes, you can. I am Chillington, the Chillmaster of Chillville. I've come here tonight to help right a wrong..."

After Chillington finished speaking, the woman, her face stained with tears and runny mascara, opened her screen door and came out onto the porch with her sad-faced son and daughter—now in their pajamas—in tow. They came down to the front walk.

Sharon looked from Glont to Tom Two to the Membrane. "I...I am truly sorry for the way we've treated you and your nephews over the years, Glont. It's horrible. I'm...I'm so ashamed."

Both Chillington and Glont did doubletakes. Head cocked quizzically, Chillington asked, "Did you really just apologize?"

"Yes. See, after we got back home tonight, I got a call from my sister. Her ten-year-old daughter, my niece, was hit by a car and killed while trick-or-treating tonight. A hit and run. As you might imagine, everybody's pretty much in shock right now. But when I got off the phone, I had something like an epiphany. I'm ashamed that it took such a horrible tragedy to make me realize it, but I now see that life is far too short for cruelty and heartlessness—that our brief time here in this world is too precious to waste on hate, ignorance, intolerance, and selfishness. So, yes, please accept my heartfelt apology. Glont, I promise to treat you and your nephews with kindness and goodwill from now on. I've also decided to teach my children about empathy and the difference between right and wrong. And I vow to never let my six-year-old daughter dress up as a slutty, sledgehammer-lickin' Miley Cyrus ever again. It'll be age-appropriate Halloween costumes from here on out! Oh, and Glont—if you don't have any plans on Sunday, I'd like to invite you and your family—your mother too—over for dinner as a gesture of goodwill and atonement."

Everyone in the woman's small audience was stunned.

"Well, how about that?" Glont said, smiling and nodding his head as he glanced from Chillington to his nephews. He turned back to Sharon. "Yeah, we'd be glad to come over for dinner on Sunday. I can't wait to tell Ma Ruth. She'll be so excited. We'll bring a dessert. What time do want us to—"

"Hey, Sharon!" Chillington interrupted, nearly shouting through clenched teeth. "Have you and your kids ever wondered what it would be like to play 'Ring Around the Rosie' with your own *goddamn, motherfucking circulatory systems?*"

"No, man!" Glont cried, stepping in front of the Chillmaster and grabbing him forcibly by the shoulders. "You promised! You swore on the fucking Bible!"

"Aw-Yeah!" Chillington said as he grappled with Glont, who tried to cover the Chillmaster's mouth with his hands.

Sharon and her children gawked at them while taking a step back, confused.

Aw-Yeah stepped out from behind a tree just as Chillington tore away from Glont and stumbled backwards.

For their part, Tom Two and The Membrane raced over to Aw-Yeah, each grabbing onto one of the mannequin's legs in an attempt to stop its approach. Barely aware of their presence, the mannequin kept moving forward, lifting them both off the ground with each step.

"Aw-Yeah!" Chillington cried. "Make these fuckers play 'Ring Around the Rosie' with their own circulatory systems!"

"Noooooo!" Glont screamed.

Sharon Simmons' entire circulatory system tore free from the rest of her body. Retaining its basic human shape, it looked as if a life-sized diagram of the human circulatory system had just leapt out of the pages of a giant anatomy textbook: connected arteries, veins, and capillaries with a still-beating heart at its center. Before the two horrified, wide-eyed children had a chance to scream, their circulatory systems forsook their bodies in the same horrific manner.

These three vein-marionettes and their erstwhile bodies formed a circle on the lawn—vein-hands joined with bloody, mangled flesh hands—while Aw-Yeah's dummy and wax doll worked the invisible puppet strings. Tom Two and The Membrane continued to pull futilely at the mannequin's legs. As the horrible circle began to turn, the dead mother and her dead children sang the dark nursery rhyme under the telekinetic direction of Aw-Yeah, though their mutilated throats, ruptured vocal cords, and shredded tongues only emitted a sort of wet, wheezy whine accompanied by a guttural croaking.

Chillington, who sat nearby in the grass clapping along, provided the missing words: "Ring around the rosie. A pocketful of posies. Ashes, Ashes, we all...fall...DOWN! Haha!"

The circle collapsed to the ground, the mother and her children's disembodied hearts beating four or five more weak beats before going permanently still.

"And we shall drink from the skulls of our enemies!" Chillington cried in a crazed voice as he shook a fist in the air. He crawled over to the circle. "And we shall eat of their flesh!" Reaching the bodies, he grabbed one of the hearts and bit into the thing like an apple. After chewing the warm heart-meat for a moment, he glanced back at Glont and his nephews. Yet again, he appeared to have forgotten they were there. Lips besmeared with crimson gore, the Chillmaster went back to looking guilty. Staring at the Lamonts, the heart fell from his trembling hand.

"Oh, dear," he said. "What have I done? I...I went too far again, didn't I? I...I'm so sorry. I promise I won't kill anyone else! And I swear I'll never tell another lie! I'll swear on the Torah! And the Koran too!"

"You're out of control, man. We're done with you. So long, Chillington."

Glont grabbed Tom Two by the hand, started jogging back to the sidewalk with The Membrane trailing closely behind them in the grass.

Still prostrate on the lawn, Chillington reached a hand up after them. "Please, just give me one more fucking chance! Pleeeeeeaaaaaaaaaaaaaaaaaaaaaaaaaaaaaaaaaaaaa-aaaaaaaaaaaaaaaaaaaaaaaaaaaaaaaaaaaaaaaaaaaaaaaaaaaaaaaa aaaaaaaaaaaaaaaaaaaaaaaaaaaaaaaaaaaaaaaaaaaaaaaaaaaaaaaa aaaaaaaaaaaaaaaaaaaaaaaaaaaaaaaaaaaaaaaaaaaaaaaaaaaaaaaa aaaassssssssssssssssssssssssssssssssssssse!!!!!!!!!!!!!!!!!!!!!!!!"

Chapter 25

They hurried back to the house, cutting through backyards to shorten the distance. On the way, Glont glanced over his shoulder a few times to see if Chillington was following them, but if the Chillmaster had decided to give chase, they'd lost him.

Just as they turned up their driveway, Glont's cell phone vibrated as a new text arrived: the first of the night. He halted, fished his phone out of his jacket's inside pocket. The text was from Amanda. It read: *Hi Glont. Hey can u come pick me up from the party and drive me home? Lance kept trying to get me to go up to his bedroom with him, but I wouldn't go. He called me a slut, fired me from Fun 4-Life, and kicked me out of his house. What an asshole!!* 😠

Glont rapidly typed a reply and sent it: *Hi Amanda. Whoa, sorry to hear u got fired. Yeah I can come get u. I'll be there in about 15 min.*

Amanda texted back a moment later: *Great! I'll be waiting out front.* 🖤😊🖤

Glont slipped his phone back into the inside pocket of his jacket. "Hey, you guys go inside. I have to go pick up Amanda at Lance's party."

Tom Two yawned wide, stretched his arms back before signing at him: *Are you coming back for our Halloween party?*

"Ya know what, guys? It's gettin' late. It's already a quarter to two in the morning. You're about to pass out,

Double T. Let's have our party tomorrow night instead. We'll get an early start on it. And we'll watch two scary movies instead of one. How's that sound?"

Tom Two pulled a sour face, crossed his arms over his chest. *But I want to come to Lance's party with you,* he signed.

Me too, The Membrane signed.

"Time for bed, Tom Two. I'm only going there to pick up Amanda, then I'm driving her home. I don't need you guys cramping my style, if ya know what I mean."

I don't know what you mean, Tom Two signed.

He means he's gonna try to play hide the salami with her, The Membrane signed.

Glont smirked, giving The Membrane the side-eye. "Well, I don't know about all that, but we'll see what happens."

Why would you want to hide a salami with her, Uncle Glont? Tom Two signed, a look of innocence pasted across his ghastly face.

He means he's gonna try to make the beast with the two backs with her, The Membrane signed.

Tom Two cocked his head to the side, now even more nonplussed. *Why would you want to make a beast with two backs, Uncle Glont?* he signed. *That sounds kinda scary.*

Come on, man! The Membrane signed, getting frustrated at Two Two's naiveté. *He means he wants to dunk his dolphin with her!*

What? Tom Two gestured, now frustrated himself. *Uncle Glont doesn't have a dolphin, you idiot!*

"Hey, don't worry about it, Tom Two. Regardless of what *I* do tonight, it's time for *you* to get to bed. Plus, I don't want you seeing any more horrible shit tonight. You're probably already gonna have nightmares for weeks about exploding heads, skeletons ripping out of their bodies, and friggin' vein-marionettes. Now get your little butt inside. You too, 'Brane!"

Chapter 26

After his nephews grudgingly went inside the house, Glont walked back to the detached garage to see if Ma Ruth's scooter was there.

It wasn't.

Man, I hope she's not getting into too much trouble with Old Crub, he thought as he glanced at her empty side of the garage. An extremely disturbing image of the filthy old man mounting his ninety-year-old, Freddy Krueger-looking mother formed in his mind's eye, and he rapidly shook his head to dispel it. He got into his Honda Disaccord, started it up, and backed out of the driveway.

As it was nearly 2:00 AM, darkness and quiet embraced the streets of Selohssa, with most of the town's lights having been turned off, the doors locked for the night. After he drove across the train tracks into the north side of town, Glont saw what at first appeared to be Freddy Krueger himself in the middle of the oncoming intersection, driving a motorcycle around in wild figure eights.

"Is that who I think it is?" he asked aloud.

A moment later, he saw it was indeed Ma Ruth on her scooter with what appeared to be a woman with long blonde hair riding in the red wagon hitched to the back. What looked like two small children sat on the woman's lap. When Glont stopped at a traffic light, he saw the blonde woman was actually a bearded old man wearing a wig and a cheap, skin-tight, low-cut miniskirt. His lips had been painted messily with garish cherry-red lipstick.

Old Crub.

Glont also noticed that what he'd first thought were children were actually inflatable life-sized dolls: a girl doll and a boy doll.

He threw the car in park, got out quickly. "Ma, what the hell are you doing?" he shouted through cupped hands to get her attention.

"Oh, hey, boy," Ma Ruth said, slurring her words. "Whuh's it look like were doin'? We're joyridin', ya big dummeh! Hee-hee-hee!" Then, she barely missed crashing into a utility pole.

Glont ran up alongside the scooter like a cowboy taming a wild horse. He grabbed the steering bar and pulled his mother's hand away from the throttle, causing the scooter to roll to a stop and bump into the curb. The woman's breath reeked of cheap booze, bubonic plague, and something else that might have been Old Crub jizz.

"You're drunk, Ma! You shouldn't be driving this thing. You guys could've gotten yourselves hurt."

"Aww, fughh you, dummeh!" She flipped him the bird with her middle-fingered Freddy blade.

"Hey, Old Crub, ya scumbag! Why are you letting my mom drive around like this?"

"Oh, he's drunker 'n me," Ma Ruth said. "Heh!"

For his part, Old Crub responded, "Aaaa-ghaarrrr-blarrrrghhhhhhhhhhh-gahhhhhhr!"

"Shit," Glont said, trying to think of what to do. A moment later, he said, "You two are coming with me. After we get Amanda, I'll take you both home."

"Alrighty," Ma Ruth said, fanning the knives of her makeshift Freddy Krueger glove. "Ya can drop us off at Old Crub's place."

"Old Crub's place is the goddamn sewer system, Ma. I'll drop Old Crub off at the sewer, but I'm taking you home!"

"Now, don't you sass me, boy! Aah'm a grown woma'. And if I wants to go home with a feller fer the night, ya best be sure that's a-what Aah'm a-gonna do, ya moron! Harrumph!"

Glont shook his head in exasperation. "Alright, Ma. I'm too tired to argue with you. I'll take you both to the sewers if that's what you fuckin' want."

First, he helped his mother out of her seat, then he went back to the wagon, gagging and wincing as he grabbed Old Crumb under his armpits and hefted him out of the wagon to his feet. He smelled like a toxic cocktail of rotten garbage and raw sewage.

The two drunken, nuthouse-bugshit insane seniors waited as Glont drove the scooter up onto the sidewalk, parking it there and taking the key with him.

"Alright, let's go," Glont said when he returned, taking Ma Ruth by the arm. "You two can ride in the backseat." He glanced over at Old Crub, gave the dude a once-over. He noticed that the two inflatable child dolls were actually attached to the front of his hot pink miniskirt, apparently as part of some Halloween get-up.

Although he was afraid to ask, Glont said, "So what the fuck are you supposed to be?"

Ma Ruth answered for him: "Ya know how lots of women's Halloween costumes these days are just sexy versions of, well, pretty much anything ya can think of? Sexy nurses and sexy policewomen and sexy nuns and sexy corn-on-the-cobs and whathaveyou?

"Yeah," Glont said.

"Well, Old Crub is Sexy Sophie's Choice. Hee-hee-hee."

The old man smiled wide, his drooling mouth a black hole rimmed with three or four cracked piss-yellow teeth.

Glont shook his head in moral disgust. "That's fucked."

Chapter 27

Glont killed the headlights when he pulled into Lance's car-filled driveway. Apparently, the party was still in full swing. If possible, he wanted to avoid any further run-ins with Lance. He parked where the driveway divided into a circle. Amanda was waiting by herself under the portico, looking hawt in her Sexy Little Red Riding Hood costume.

"You two wait here," Glont said. He glanced in the rearview mirror to witness the disturbing sight of Freddy Krueger sloppily making out with Sexy Sophie's Choice.

"Gross!" Glont muttered as he got out of the car. He walked briskly up to the house, and Amanda came down the steps when she saw him, meeting him in the driveway.

"Your poor lip!" she said, placing a hand on his cheek and leaning in to get a better look. "How long do you have to keep the stitches in?"

"I'm not sure."

"Didn't the doctor tell you?"

"I didn't go to a doctor. It's kind of a long story. I'll tell you about it later if you want." He took her by the forearm. "C'mon. Let's get outta here."

As they started to walk back to his car, the muted sound of the party surged in volume when the front door of the house opened behind them.

"Well, well, well," Lance said. "Look who's back. If it isn't My Tiny Little Weak Bitch, the prodigal shithead returned."

Glont halted, turned around. Lance's crown, scepter, and robe were gone. His thick hair was disheveled, and lipstick stains dappled his neck and chin. Barely holding onto the neck of a half-full bottle of beer in one hand, a drunken glaze in his eyes, he waddled down the front steps. A stream of equally wasted party guests followed him out of the house. Guests continued to pour out of the front door onto the veranda even after Lance stopped at the bottom of the steps. Among them were many of Glont's coworkers, including Sam the bouncing clown, who was now dressed in an offensive, culturally appropriated Sexy Indian Seductress costume, complete with redface and a headdress. Glont's big baby of a floor manager, Marty, was there, too, dressed as an offensive, culturally appropriated Chinaman, complete with yellowface, a wide Asian rice hat, and chopsticks.

"So I guess there's no TERROR MANNEQUIN hiding out at Fallingwater after all, huh?" Lance asked.

Glont didn't answer.

"Still, that was a pretty rad idea to set you guys up so you had to go reverse trick-or-treating out there tonight—whoever idea it was. But as it turns out, I'm glad you didn't die out there. You know why?"

"Fuck you," Glont said.

"Because now you can die here! Or else get the fuck outta town!" Lance lifted a sausagey finger of condemnation at Glont. "I, Lance Montgomery, your goodly king, do hereby command thee to bite off thy bottom lip while plucking thine own eyes out of thy face! There's no saving you this time. If you don't comply, then say goodbye to your job, asshole. Ahh-ha-ha-ha…"

Before Glont had a chance to respond, who should step out from behind a parked SUV and stand midway between him and Lance? Why, it was none other than Chillington, the Chillmaster of Chillville!!!

"You got that wrong, son," the Chillmaster said to Lance. "I'm afraid it's *you* who's about to say goodbye. And not just to your job. To your fucking life!"

Eyes squinting, brow knitting, Lance tilted his head quizzically. "And who the fuck are you supposed to be?"

"I'm Chillington, the Chillmaster of Chillville."

Lance glowered at the Chillmaster for a moment before speaking. "The Chillmaster of Chillville? Pfft! You look more like the Turdmaster of Fagtown to me. Now, get the fuck off my property before I knock your goddamn head off, oldster."

"Aw-Yeah!" the Chillmaster called as he raised his hand, beckoning the creature to come forth from behind him. Aw-Yeah waddled out into view from the shadows, halting at its master's side. The crowd gathered behind Lance uttered a collective gasp.

"What in tarnation is that?" Ma Ruth asked, her Freddy face peeking around Glont's shoulder, startling him. Glont turned around to see both her and Old Crub standing behind him.

"Ma, I told you two to stay in the goddamn car!"

"What is that thing?" Lance uttered, his face paling. "Is that…fucking TERROR MANNEQUIN?"

"Shut him up, Aw-Yeah," Chillington said.

As the dummy reached its free arm toward Lance, the man went bug-eyed with panic and terror, the muscles of his arms and legs gone rigid under Aw-Yeah's paralysis spell.

"But to answer your question—no, that's not TERROR MANNEQUIN. TERROR MANNEQUIN was destroyed long ago. This is Aw-motherfuckin'-Yeah." Chillington turned to Glont. "By the way, you might as well know the truth. I was the one who took down the barbed wire and all the KEEP OUT signs."

"What?" Glont said. "But why?"

"All the things I told you about myself were true, but I didn't tell you everything, like how my violent fantasies started to change over time, how I also started to fantasize about maiming and murdering good people—innocents. At one point, the darkness took full control over me, like a demonic spirit. It made me take down the barbed wire and all those signs to lure trick-or-treaters back to Fallingwater. I was going to have Aw-Yeah kill everyone who came through! Luckily, only you guys made the trip. And when you arrived, something brought me out of the dark place I'm in, or at least partway out. I'm not positive, but I think it was being in the presence of Tom Two—of bearing witness to his purity, innocence, and chillness of spirit. Anyway, now I must cleanse myself of the last bit of darkness within me by making this final human sacrifice, one that is truly deserved."

Chillington turned to Lance. "Hey, asshole. Bite off thy bottom lip and pluck thy eyes out thy face! Aw-Yeah, make him do so! But slowly so he suffers! Oh, and make him stuff his eyeballs up his ass, too! Shit, might as well have him rip his balls off, too, and insert them into his empty eye sockets. I mean, why not, right? Heh-heh!"

Raising his fingers to his eyes, Lance sucked his lower lip into his mouth.

Despite hating Lance with every fiber of his being and knowing he totally deserved what he was getting, Glont had no interest in witnessing the gory spectacle that was about to unfold before them.

"Let's get out of here," he said under his breath to Amanda, grabbing both her and Ma Ruth by their arms to sneak away. They resumed walking hurriedly back to the car.

"Now, you let go of me!" Ma Ruth protested. "I wanna see Lance stick his peepers up his butt!"

Smiling manically, Chillington glanced over his shoulder. "Not so fast, Glont. Aw-Yeah, freeze him!"

As soon as the command was uttered, Glont released Amanda's and Ma Ruth's arms and turned in place to face the house. No longer in control of his body from the mouth down, his eyes darted about in panic.

"This one's for you, my friend," Chillington said. "You need to watch this. I mean, this fucker's been tormenting and harassing you your entire life. Pantsing you. Locking you in lockers. Beating your skinny ass. Making you eat dog turds in the schoolyard. Humiliating you. And twice tonight he and his asshole friends were ready to watch you bleed to death out here on this driveway. Well, I have a funny feeling that Lance's bullying days are over. See, I suspect there's little else more permanently subduing to a person than being forced to gouge their own eyes out and stuff them up their ass before ripping their nuts off and sticking them into their empty eye sockets!"

A mixture of tears and blood leaked out of Lance's eyes as his fingers dug deeper into his orbits, twin rivulets running down his cheeks to meet in the cleft of his chiseled chin.

Word of what was happening quickly passed from the front of the crowd to the back, and more people came out of the house to see what the commotion was all about. Guests began to panic. Two of Lance's douchebag frat boy toadies came to his side. One was dressed up as a pregnant nun, the other as a hillbilly having sex with a sheep.

"What the fuck is wrong with you, bro?" the pregnant nun asked. He grabbed onto Lance's left arm while the hillbilly grabbed onto the right one. They pulled with all their strength in a futile attempt to get their bro to take his fingers out of his eye sockets.

"Aw-Yeah!" Chillington said. "Make these two assholes rip each other's faces off and feed them to each other while they—oh, I don't know—engage in Irish step dancing to the best of their ability."

Lance's pals immediately released him, then went at each other's faces.

Just then, Ma-He's-Makin'-Eyes-At-Me appeared at the edge of the confused crowd, which continued to grow on the veranda and spill out into the driveway. As usual, she was dressed as Dorothy from *The Wizard of Oz*. Glont noticed her immediately. He tried to break free of the paralysis spell, to turn around and warn Amanda just in case she wasn't in the know about the danger of Ma-He's-Makin'-Eyes-At-Me and her diabolical mother. However, he couldn't break free from the unholy magic.

Chillington noticed her, too. He took a few steps forward to get a better look. "Well, look at you," he called to her. "Great costume. Your dress actually falls below the knee. Just like the real thing. Hey, kudos for being the first woman I've seen tonight who's not dressed up as the 'sexy' version of something or other—the little sluts!"

An attractive woman at the front of crowd then gave him the finger. "Hey, fuck you, old man. Don't you know it's archaic to slut-shame people?" She was dressed up as a Sexy 9/11 Twin Tower (her costume consisted of a low-cut, cleavage-showing, skintight, gray bodysuit printed with a grid-like pattern of windows, the words "NORTH TOWER" sewn across her jutting bosom in white block letters). Her equally offended friend stood beside her dressed in the same getup except for the words "SOUTH TOWER" embroidered under her cleavage.

Somewhat smitten with Dorothy, Chillington ignored those assholes. "And you even look like Judy Garland in the face! Anyone ever tell you that, miss?"

That's when Ma-He's-Makin'-Eyes-At-Me stepped forward, pointed at Chillington, and recited that dreaded string of words: "*Ma, he's makin' eyes at me!*"

Oh, no! Glont thought.

A beat later, the tall shrubs that flanked the eastern wing of the mansion parted to let through an invisible bulk, a deep growl rumbling in its throat. It trampled over a parked Jaguar two cars down from where Chillington stood, the car's windows shattering outward as the roof caved in.

"Shit," Chillington muttered, only now recalling how Glont had told him about Ma-He's-Makin'-Eyes-At-Me and her mother—the invisible, monstrous Mrs. Smith. Just as he was about to run like hell the other way, the invisible horror knocked him off his feet and onto his back on the concrete. He screamed as something sharp ripped through his Bob Ross t-shirt to carve a red slash across his belly. At the same time, something like a frenzied horde of tiny invisible mouths commenced biting into his clothing and at his exposed skin.

As Aw-Yeah's number one duty was to protect its master, the dummy and the wax doll released their sorcerous holds on Lance, his two friends, and Glont in order to assist Chillington.

Lance's lower lip hanging inside-out on his bloody chin and barely attached to his face, he sank to his knees and pulled his fingers out of his ruptured eye sockets. His two now-faceless buddies ceased force-feeding one another their own faces and Irish step dancing to the shrill music of their own agonized shrieks.

Glont turned to Amanda, moved in front of her to block her view of the scene. "Hey, see that chick dressed as Dorothy? Don't look her in the eye for more than a second or two. If she catches anyone doing so, she—"

"She tells her invisible monster of a mother," Amanda interrupted. "And the mother tears them apart, just like she's doing to your friend there. Yeah, my realtor warned me about her before I moved into my house."

Aw-Yeah's Chicken McNugget head tilted in confusion, and its little mouth opened in a shocked o-shape as it gawked at its master thrashing about on the driveway. A moment later, the thumb, index finger, and middle finger on Chillington's left hand disappeared in a spray of blood as an unseen mouth bit them off with a snap.

"It's fucking invisible!" Chillington screamed at Aw-Yeah, his face a bloody, grated mess. "Use your power! Turn this fucking thing inside out! Make it stick its invisible fucking head up its invisible fucking ass, Aw-Yeah! Ahaaaeeeeeeehhh…"

The dummy reached with its free hand at the general area above Chillington, the space presumably occupied by the invisible attacker. Its hand fanned out, fingers dancing, as it attempted to drive its telekinetic hooks into her, but its power had no effect because it could not see its target. Not knowing what else to do, Aw-Yeah dove onto the unseen beast. The mannequin freed up its left arm and grabbed onto the thing's back. The dummy—now unseated, the mannequin's hand still embedded in its back—clamped onto the beast's unseen hide with its free arm. While the mannequin and dummy held on tight, the wax doll and the voodoo doll beat the thing with their free limbs. For its part, the Chicken McNugget head repeatedly headbutted the invisible monster. From the perspective of all onlookers, Aw-Yeah appeared to float four or five feet in the air above the Chillmaster as the wax doll, the voodoo doll, and the Chicken McNugget struck nothing but air.

Something quite incredible then happened: Since Aw-Yeah and Mrs. Smith were both supernatural entities born of dark magic, their physical contact acted somewhat like an electrical short, shutting off both Mrs. Smith's invisibility and Aw-Yeah's telekinetic power.

The crowded gasped.

Above Chillington's struggling form slouched a creature with the muscular body of a werewolf that was over eight feet tall when it stood upright on its powerful hind legs.

Its warped head was that of a demonic clown—waxy-white face, coal-black eyes ringed with blue, yawning blood-red mouth stretching from misshapen ear to misshapen ear. Crowning the demonic clown head was a hissing, writhing mass of snakes like a gorgon's, except each serpent terminated in a smaller copy of the demonic clown head. These plumb-sized demonic clown heads were themselves crowned with snakes the size of earthworms, which themselves ended in even tinier, snake-capped demonic clown heads. Like mirrors within mirrors, this fractal pattern went on forever, the demonic clown heads and snakes disappearing into infinity.

For arms, the monster had two 5-foot-long juvenile great white sharks, each attached by its tail to one of the massive werewolf shoulders. Orbiting the beast like angry wasps around a ruptured nest were dozens of zombie air-piranha, though most of these flying, undead fish were busy picking away at the fallen Chillmaster. Though Aw-Yeah continued to hold onto to Mrs. Smith's back via the mannequin and the dummy, and though the wax doll and voodoo doll kept beating her with their free limbs, Mrs. Smith seemed unaware of Aw-Yeah's puny presence.

Glont turned away from the struggle, dragging Amanda and Ma Ruth with him back to the car. Amanda got into the passenger seat and shut the door while Glont helped his mother into the backseat. The throng of panicked party guests began to disperse, some running for the neighbor's yards, others giving the now visible Mrs. Smith, Aw-Yeah, and Chillington a wide berth as they ran for their cars in the driveway. Glont glanced back at the chaos as he opened the car door to get in. He spotted Old Crub several feet away from the struggle tearing pieces of his face off and devouring them while his gangly legs kicked about in some sort of terrible imitation of an Irish jig. And he was doing so of his own volition! Lance's two buddies, who had both collapsed to bleed out onto the driveway, had apparently inspired the nuthouse-bugshit insane old man to imitate them.

And peeking out from behind a parked car not far from Old Crub were Tom Two and The Membrane!

"Shit!" Glont said. He lowered his head into the car. "Tom Two and The Membrane are up there. Wait here." Leaving the car door open, he ran back toward the house.

"What the hell are you guys doing?" he yelled when he reached them, grabbing Tom Two by the shoulders and turning him away from the terrible spectacle. "I told you guys to stay at home! You're supposed to be in bed, Tom Two."

The Membrane left me all alone in the house, Tom Two signed. *I was scared, so I got out of bed when I heard him leave, and I followed him here.*

Man, I was just hoping to score a piece of ass at this party, The Membrane signed.

"Christ. C'mon, let's get outta of here!" Glont said.

But before he could reach down and sweep Tom Two up onto his shoulder like Tiny Tim, Lance came up from behind him, shoved him hard. When Glont spun around to face him, Lance sucker-punched him in the face, laying him out on the ground and causing him to black out for a second. When he came to, Glont was sprawled out on his stomach on the driveway, his nose bleeding and broken from smacking against the pavement. As Lance fell upon him, Glont rolled onto his back to see the man's disfigured face—bulging, bloody eyes and flappy, mostly detached lip—hovering above his own.

"Your fucking friend mutilated me!" he spat, grabbing Glont's head in both hands as if to crush it. "But he didn't finish what he started. I still have my eyes, see? Looks like you're the one who's gonna get his eyes shoved up his ass tonight after all."

Glont grabbed Lance's wrists, pushing back as the man's thumbs edged closer toward his eyes. A beat later, The Membrane slid up Lance's back and enveloped his head. Lance's hands immediately abandoned Glont's face as he clutched at The Membrane in an attempt to pull the thing off, but the creature tightened its grip, its outermost edges wrapping around Lance's neck to choke him, suffocating him while its secreted digestive juices ate away at the man's skin.

Still disoriented from getting punched in the nose, Glont took the opportunity flip over on his belly and crawl out from underneath Lance. As he did so, he found himself looking beyond the landscaped circle enclosed by the driveway to the expansive lawn that separated the mansion from the street. The wind picked up, and pockets of dry leaves skittered across the short-clipped grass, momentarily mesmerizing Glont in his delirium, causing him to think of herds of tiny wild horses. And there, out near the middle of the lawn, he espied in his blurry vision a white, oval-shaped form. Something about the thing gave him pause. He squinted to see it better, trying to discern what the shape was. Whatever it was, it slowly grew as it approached the house.

Just as Glont crawled out from under Lance, one of the demonic clown-headed serpents that grew out of Mrs. Smith's head finally noticed Aw-Yeah clinging to her back. It sidewinded its way down the beast's spine, and its terrible, little chalk-white face and round, red nose stopped an inch short of headbutting the Chicken McNugget head. The clown head's red lips peeled back to reveal jagged, nail-like teeth lining its mouth, before it pulled back a few inches to strike at the McNugget head like lightning. However, its aim was off: its teeth closed around Aw-Yeah's spring-neck, which snapped as the clown headed-snake retracted like a whip.

The McNugget's face scrunched into an "oh no!" expression as it tumbled to the ground. At that same moment, the ventriloquist dummy's eyes rolled back into its head, and the wax doll's orange-glowing pupils dimmed to black. The mannequin's right arm slid limply out of the dummy's back, the dummy's right arm withdrew from the wax doll, and the wax doll's right arm pulled out of the voodoo doll, whereupon the voodoo doll released the crank of the now unoccupied jack-in-the-box. The mannequin and the dummy then released their holds on the monster—Aw-Yeah's separated pieces fell into a pile on the driveway. When the physical contact between Aw-Yeah and Mrs. Smith broke, the monster once again turned invisible.

Several feet away, Lance finally managed to pry The Membrane from his head and toss the thing away. Steaming in the cool night air, the man's entire head and neck had been stripped down to quivering, beet-red muscle, his eyeballs flashing white with terror and agony in the melted wreckage of his face. Only after he took in and released the deep breath for which he'd fought so hard did Lance commence screaming in agony.

Still prostrate on the concrete, Glont continued to stare at the approaching pale form out on the windswept lawn. He realized it was some sort of humanoid figure, its gait stiff and mechanical, and that it appeared to be carrying something. It reached the other side of the circle driveway, began to cross the landscaped circle. That's when Glont realized what the thing was.

"Holy shit," he whispered.

He scrambled up onto his hands and knees, hauled himself upright, and turned to face the others.

"Hey, everyone—it's fucking TERROR MANNEQUIN!" he shouted through cupped hands, trying to be heard over Lance's terrible shrieking and the screams of the many confused and terrified party guests.

The pale mannequin, its mouth agape and eyes wide open in self-aware horror, moved its hand inside the grinning dummy's back, causing it to do the same to the glowing-eyed wax doll, which induced the faceless voodoo doll to turn the crank on the wooden box.

"It's TERROR MANNEQUIN!" Glont cried again. "Don't look at the jack-in-the-box!" But his pleas and the tinny music-box notes of "Pop! Goes the Weasel" were lost in the chaos and cacophony of the surrounding mass exodus.

Pop!

Still screaming from getting his face dissolved off, Lance was the first to look over in the direction of TERROR MANNEQUIN, the wooden box now sprung open. He immediately clutched at his chest, his heart collapsing in on itself and metamorphosing into a Totino's pizza roll while his brain melted and transmogrified into a mixture of dogshit, worms, and maggots. His eyes swelled up like water balloons and burst, allowing the dogshit, maggots, and worms to extrude from his eye sockets and slide down his cheeks—basically big, brown dogshit-tears of death—before the man pitched forward onto the liquified front of his skull.

Just as Lance's heart collapsed, Old Crub was the second person to see TERROR MANNEQUIN. He ceased eating his own face and dancing to fall to his knees and suffer the same fate. Dozens of guests collided and stumbled over one another as they shoved their way out of the house and down the front steps. Falling to the ground, they too beheld whatever unimaginable horror had sprung from the box.

Still facing away from the thing, Glont went over to Tom Two, The Membrane, Ma Ruth, and Amanda, who were huddled together on the driveway. Several dead or dying bodies lay scattered around the group, dogshit oozing from their skulls. Apparently, Ma Ruth and Amanda had left the car when they saw Lance attacking Glont. Luckily, they had been close enough to hear and heed Glont's warning in time, so that each of them had covered their eyes with their hands. Though The Membrane had neither eyes, heart, nor brain, it had erred on the side of caution by scrunching up into a tight ball to cloak its weird eyeless sense of sight.

"Glont!" Chillington's hoarse voice called from off to his right. He turned to see a bloody, lacerated arm reaching up towards him.

"Wait here!" he said as he grasped Amanda and Ma Ruth each by the shoulder. "I'll be right back. Keep your eyes covered until I say otherwise." He made his way over to what was left of the Chillmaster, quickly stepping over several bodies while holding his right hand to the side of his face like a visor so he wouldn't see TERROR MANNEQUIN.

Mrs. Smith had retreated back behind the pines, apparently content to leave Chillington for dead without finishing the job. Not long for this world, all that remained of the man was his right arm and a flayed head attached to an equally peeled half-torso. One of his eyes was gone. Everything below his ribcage abdomen was basically just a big red splat, and a trail of gore led several feet back to the spot where Mrs. Smith had brought him down. Chillington's head was propped up against the tire of a parked Cadillac Escalade. When Glont knelt down by him, Chillington grabbed him by the breast of his jacket with his remaining limb, pulled him in closer.

"Glont," he croaked "I'm…I'm sorry that I killed those people earlier tonight. Especially those two kids."

Glont was silent for a moment, unsure of what to say. "Hey, man. Um, like, it's okay. I mean, who knows? Maybe those two kids would have grown up to be serial killers or something."

"But what if they'd grown up to be great artists or philanthropists or doctors that cured cancer?"

"Well, I don't think it matters, man. I mean, it wasn't really your fault. Like you said, you had this dark unchill energy inside you, basically controlling you, ya know?"

"Aw-Yeah's head…it rolled under this car. I can't reach it. Can you grab it for me, muh…muh…my tiny little son?"

"Of course." Glont got down on his belly, peered under the SUV, where he saw a small dark lump sitting under the center of the vehicle. He reached under as far as his arm would go, straining until his fingers closed around the thing. He pushed himself back up onto his knees, set the McNugget in Chillington's extended bloody palm. As soon at the thing came into contact with its master, the dark lines of its face once again kindled with ember-orange light.

"Listen," Chillington said before hacking up a thick plug of clotting blood. "Despite my transgressions, I'm still the Chillmaster of Chillville. I want you to go to Chillville and tell the chillagers that, just before my death, I appointed Tom Two to be the new Chillmaster of Chillville. That is, of course, if he wants to take the job. If he does, he can bring you and your family to live there with him if you like. Please do this. It's my…my dying wish."

Glont was taken aback. "Wow. Yeah, of course. I'll tell 'em, man. And, um, thank you."

"Now, move to the side so I can finish this," the former Chillmaster of Chillington said as he held the McNugget above his head. Aw-Yeah's face now burned brighter with golden light. Chillington cocked his arm back, closed his one remaining eye.

Glont had a pretty good idea of what was about to happen. He got up and sidestepped away from Chillington with his back to TERROR MANNEQUIN.

Chillington opened his eye to a slit, immediately sighting his target not twenty feet away before him. Just as his heart began to shrink in his chest and just as his cerebellum transmuted into worm-riddled dogshit, he tossed Aw-Yeah's head at TERROR MANNEQUIN, his aim true.

Flying in a high arc toward its target, Aw-Yeah spoke one last time: "Awwwwwwwwwwwwwwwwwwwwww-wwwwwwwwwwwwwwwwwwwwwwwwwwwwwwwww wwwwwwwwwwwwwwwwwwwwwwwwwwwwwwwww wwwwwwwwwwwwwwwwwwwwwww Yeah!"

Chapter 28

A bright red light flashed behind Glont, momentarily illuminating the pine trees in front of him, followed by a blast of heat that nearly knocked him off his feet, thrusting him into the side of the Escalade. After the light faded away, he slowly turned around. A low mound of gray ash remained at the edge of the lawn where TERROR MANNEQUIN had stood a moment ago—a plume of gray smoke twisted up into the air from the mound to break apart in the wind.

Glont rushed over to the others. The heat blast had knocked Tom Two, Ma Ruth, and Amanda on their asses. They were just getting up from the ground, Amanda helping Ma Ruth.

"Is everyone okay?" Glont asked.

"I think so," Amanda said. Tom Two gave a thumbs up.

"What the heck happened?" Ma Ruth asked.

"Chillington threw Aw-Yeah's Chicken McNugget head at TERROR MANNEQUIN. Because Aw-Yeah was the cree-craw that had been specifically summoned to destroy TERROR MANNEQUIN, they annihilated each other on contact."

Glont turned in place to survey the gory scene. Dozens of costumed dead bodies littered the veranda, the front steps, and the top of the driveway. From what he could see, they were the sole survivors. The air reeked of ripe dogshit.

Amanda rushed forward, embraced Glont tightly. She pressed the side of her face against his chest, her head fitting perfectly under his chin. "You saved us!"

"Well, Chillington actually saved us. But, yeah, I guess I helped."

"You warned us to close our eyes," Amanda said as she released him.

"Fuck, I just wish more people would have heard me."

A twig snapped nearby, causing everyone to look towards the tree-lined side of the driveway. That's when Ma-He's-Makin'-Eyes-At-Me emerged from between two pines, halting at the edge of the driveway about two car lengths down. Everyone immediately redirected their eyes from her face when they saw her.

"Oh, you made it," Glont said, looking down at her ruby slippers.

With her brow knitted in a sharp "v" and her lips smushed in a pouty frown, Ma-He's-Makin'-Eyes-At-Me raised a condemning index finger at Amanda. *"Ma...she's makin' eyes at me!"*

Aghast because her line of vision had been nowhere near Ma-He's-Makin'-Eyes-At-Me's face, Amanda shouted, "What! That's not true! I completely looked away the second I saw you!"

Still pointing at her, Ma-He's-Makin'-Eyes-At-Me repeated the awful death sentence, but louder this time: *"Ma, she's makin' eyes at me!"*

"No! no!" Glont cried as he got in front of Amanda and held his arms out to defend her. "That's not fair. She didn't fuckin' look at you, and you know it! Take it back, Ma-He's-Makin'-Eyes-At-Me!" He glanced back at Amanda. "You're sure you didn't look her in the eye for more than a second, right?"

"Of course I'm sure!" she said, tears springing from her eyes.

But Ma-He's-Makin'-Eyes-At-Me was relentless. "*Ma, she's makin' eyes at me!*" she said a third time.

Glont was in the middle of yelling, "Run, Amanda!" when the invisible beast knocked him out of her way, sending him tumbling onto the concrete.

Amanda screamed, but her cries stopped abruptly when she appeared to levitate three feet off the ground, her Sexy Little Red Riding Hood cloak flapping wildly in the wind. Apparently, the beast had lifted her up by the neck.

"Now we'll see how *red* this Sexy Little Red Riding Hood really is!" Ma-He's-Makin'-Eyes-At-Me! said before laughing maniacally.

"Make her stop!" Glont yelled at his ex-girlfriend as he pushed himself up off the ground.

"No! You're *my* boyfriend, Glont. And she tried to steal you away from me, the slut!"

"I'm not your boyfriend! We broke up ages ago! You know what? Just, wait! Okay, okay. I'll be your boyfriend. Just please let her go! She's innocent! Please don't fucking kill her!"

Amanda's ripped-off, balled-up face then pegged Glont in the forehead like a warm, wet rag, painting his face scarlet with hot blood. The rubbery thing opened as it fell onto the concrete—a ghastly oval flap of skin with eyeholes, nostril holes, and a mouth hole—Amanda's luscious lips still intact.

"Fuck," Glont muttered as he stared down at the thing, clutching his head in both hands while Mrs. Smith continued to flay, eviscerate, and skeletonize Amanda in his peripheral vision.

"Glont!" Ma Ruth screamed. "Get Tom Two! He's running out to the street!"

Glont turned to his mother and saw that Tom Two was no longer at her side. She pointed over at the front lawn and cried "Get the baby!" just like Mrs. Creed did in *Pet Sematary*.

He followed her finger and, sure enough, there was Tom Two—bareheaded—out near the middle of the front yard chasing after his sombrero. A gust had apparently knocked it off his head. Still propelled along by the wind, the hat skated and tumbled across the lawn toward the street.

Glont took off running as fast as he could.

"Get the baby!" Ma Ruth cried again, hobbling after Glont as if she could help him.

"Double T!" Glont shouted after he crossed the landscaped island and reached the front yard proper. "Stop, dude! Let the hat go!"

Tom Two apparently did not hear his uncle—he kept running after his hat.

Glont was gaining on him, but Tom Two was a quick and determined little bugger. Nearly halfway to the street, Glont spotted headlights coming around the bend in the road.

It was a semi-truck.

And it was approaching fast.

In fact, remember that truck that ran over Gage Creed in *Pet Sematary*? Well, this was the exact same red Peterbilt eighteen-wheeler and the exact same driver. Can you fucking believe it? How could that asshole still be allowed to drive a rig? Yet here he was barreling down Diamond Boi Drive in his rig at two-thirty in the morning on the day after Halloween in Selohssa, Pennsylvania. And he was drunk as shit to boot. I mean, what kind of bullshit is that? In fact, it makes me so angry that I'm tearing out what little hair remains on my head with my right hand as I type these very words with my left hand, and I'm about ready to chuck my laptop across the room here in the fucking Taco Hell where I'm writing.

Anyway, Tom Two's sombrero tumbled out into the middle of the street, where it finally rolled to a stop. Glont was about thirty feet back when Tom Two scampered across the tree lawn and over the curb.

At this point, everything was in dramatic slo-mo.

"Tom, stop!" Glont cried out as he pumped his legs and arms harder. He stumbled, lost his footing, fell to the ground just shy of the sidewalk—just like that idiot Louis Creed did in *Pet Sematary*.

Had the potentially eons-old part of Tom Two been more dominant at this moment, he would surely have been more mindful of the cries of his uncle and grandmother, of the semi's screeching brakes and shrieking air horn. But as it happened, the two-year-old part was dominant, so that Tom Two remained intent on his simple purpose. The newly appointed Chillmaster of Chillville—though he would never know he had attained that singular, illustrious honor—

stopped beside his big hat, stooped down, snatched it up, and put it right back where it belonged on his big, lightbulb-shaped head.

And even as he looked up into the bright, yellow eyes of the oncoming semi, Tom Two still trusted that, despite a Halloween filled with unkind people doing unkind things, buckets of blood and guts, monsters (both visible and invisible), exploding heads, skeletons and circulatory systems tearing out of people's bodies, dogshit and worms oozing out of eye sockets, and beating hearts shriveling up into Totino's pizza rolls, the world was still more or less a good place.

Epilogue

Tom Two's ill-attended graveside funeral service took place on a miserable, dismal, cold-ass, gray-ass, rainy-ass, shit-morning five days later. Present were the officiating priest, Glont, Ma Ruth, The Membrane, Ma-He's-Makin'-Eyes-At-Me, and her invisible mother. All the visible attendees were dressed appropriately in black. Even The Membrane was draped in a somber black cloth that Ma Ruth had trimmed to fit its shape the previous night. Tom Two's tombstone was inscribed thusly:

HERE LIES

TOM TWO

BELOVED NEPHEW, GRAND NEPHEW, BROTHER, & THE GODDAMN, MOTHER-FUCKING CHILLMASTER OF MOTHER-FUCKING CHILLVILLE (IF FOR BUT A MOMENT)

???? – 2019

RIP

Near the end of the service, a black stretch limo edged up the drive and parked behind the hearse. A chauffer got out, opened the passenger door, and the screaming figure from Edvard Munch's *The Scream* stepped out. Everyone watched in amazement as he approached the gravesite.

"I'm sorry for your loss, everyone," the figure said in a heavy Norwegian accent. He pulled a rose from the flower arrangement and tossed it into the grave, where Tom Two's diminutive coffin had just been lowered. He took a step back, folded his arms near his waist, and respectfully bowed his big lightbulb-shaped head.

Glont eyeballed him quizzically. "Um, are you who I think you are?"

"Probably. I'm the screaming figure from Munch's famous painting. Like the painting, my name is also The Scream. I am Tom Two's father."

The other mourners emitted a collective gasp.

"I...I felt his death. Felt it kind of like a disturbance in The Force, I guess you could say. So as soon as I was able to, I climbed out of *The Scream*—as in the painting—at the National Gallery in Oslo, Norway, and booked a flight to the U.S. It was a long trip. I'm glad I made it here before the funeral ended."

He reached into a pocket in his sooty robe, pulled out his iPhone XS to check the time.

"Ah, unfortunately, I must be off. Wish I could stay longer, but my flight to London leaves in less than two hours. The director at the gallery wants me back as soon as possible. I guess the Queen of England, the Prince of Liechtenstein, and the Grand Duke of Luxembourg are in town this weekend and will be visiting the museum. As you might well imagine, the museum's most popular attraction—Edvard Munch's *The Scream*—is somewhat uninteresting when I'm not there."

Glont's mind buzzed with dozens of questions for The Scream. *Did he know how or why Tom Two never aged past two years? How old was he himself? Who was Tom Two's mother? And how the hell did he come to life and leave the famous painting he lived in?*

But he didn't ask The Scream any of these things. Instead, he asked the only fucking question that motherfucking mattered: "Hey, if you're really his dad, then where the fuck have you been all these years, G?"

The Scream was taken aback. "Why, in the Munch painting, of course. I mean, that's my job. I'm The Scream. That's what I do."

"But you had a son, dude. He didn't even know about you. You never visited. Never sent him a dime. You never called him. Never even wrote him a lousy letter!"

"You don't understand. You don't know what it's like being an iconic figure in a world-famous, priceless piece of art. Let's just say that I'm very, very busy."

Ma Ruth said, "Apparently not too busy to sneak out of that dang picture and knock up some little hussy somewhere, ya screamin' rascal, you!"

"Yeah," Glont said, getting in The Scream's face.

"I...I have to get going now," The Scream said nervously as he backed away from Glont.

Glont took a step toward him, The Membrane sliding alongside him. "Why, you're nothing but a deadbeat dad!" he said before he and The Membrane pounced on him.

They beat The Scream's deadbeat-dad ass good. In fact, they beat him down to a pile of oil paints, tempera, pastels, and cardboard, effectively destroying him.

Nowadays, if you visit the National Gallery in Oslo, you can still see Munch's iconic painting. You can see the swirling red-orange sky, the blue-black fjord, the fenced-in road, and the two figures in the background, but the painting's superstar is conspicuously absent. As such, the painting sucks a big, blue, spiked dick now, so much so that museum had to change its name from *The Scream* to *The Shit*.

***

About two months after Tom Two's funeral, The Membrane starved to death.

See, not everyone knows this, but apparently Totino's food products—namely Party Pizzas and Pizza Rolls—were actually made by a guy whose name was actually Totino, kind of like Prince or Madonna. One night, your boy Totino went fucking nuthouse-bugshit insane, locked himself in his factory, and set the place ablaze. The building burned to the ground with him in it. No more Totino meant no more Totino's Party Pizzas and Pizza Polls, and the world's remaining stock of those products depleted in no time.

If you recall, Totino's Party Pizzas were the only food The Membrane ever ate. When there were no more to be had, Glont tried buying other types of frozen pizzas for the thing—DiGiorno, Tombstone, Red Barron, Tony's, etc.—but The Membrane refused to even try them. Desperate to get the thing to eat something—anything—Glont tried feeding it various types of other food—steak, burgers, fries, chicken, seafood, candy, cookies, cakes, pies, etc.—but The Membrane just wasn't having it. Basically, the thing went on a hunger strike because it was so damn pissed off that Totino's Party Pizzas were gone forever. All Glont, Ma Ruth, and Ma-He's-Makin'-Eyes-At-Me could do was watch as it wasted away on their living room floor, basically shrinking and drying up into a dead, white, dried-out piece of dogshit.

(Oh, realizing Ma-He's-Makin'-Eyes-At-Me would never let him get a new girlfriend, Glont decided to accept his lot in life and got back together with her shortly after Tom Two's death. They were soon married, whereupon Glont's new bride and his invisible monstrosity of a mother-in-law moved into the Lamont house.)

Anyway, they buried The Membrane in a grave next to Tom Two's. In its will, The Membrane had insisted that it be laid to rest in a stately mausoleum, the cost of which should be no less than $350,000. However, should funds not allow for such a lavish place of interment, the will indicated that a towering, phallic obelisk cut from the finest Italian marble available at a cost of no less than $150,000 would suffice as The Membrane's grave marker, so long as the obelisk was the largest gravestone in the cemetery. Obviously, the financially-strapped Lamonts could not afford to honor either of these requests. Instead, The Membrane's tombstone was a common cinder block. It was basically a shitstone. Nevertheless, per the instructions outlined in its will, and though the epitaph was a boldfaced lie, the marker was inscribed thusly:

HERE LIES

THE MEMBRANE

THE THING NABBED MORE ASS THAN A CHINESE ZOO

???? – 2020

RIP

***

Despite great protests from her son, Ma Ruth left the Lamont family ancestral home a few weeks after The Membrane died in order to pursue an acting career in the burgeoning geriatric/quicksand/Freddy Krueger fetish porn industry in Hollywood. Who knew that was even a thing? But sure enough, this particular newfangled niche Internet porn category that married the three usually separate geriatric, quicksand, and Freddy Kruger fetish porn categories into one fucked-up thing had been gaining lots of Internet clicks over the past few years.

The morning she left, Glont and Ma-He's-Makin'-Eyes-At-Me went outside to see her off.

"But, Ma," he said as she slowly got onto her scooter, her travel tote already strapped onto the back of it, "what kind of life is this for a ninety-year-old woman with bubonic plague and leprosy? Shouldn't you just enjoy the time you have left on this planet here at home?"

"I've spent my whole dang life in this here house. It's high time I had some excitement and adventure, don'tcha think? Anyhow, I'll just be gone a few months. I always did want to be an actress in Hollywood. My new boss says he's gonna make me a star!"

Ma Ruth achieved her Warholian fifteen minutes of fame, even if it was in the geriatric/quicksand/Freddy Krueger fetish porn industry. And she returned home in a few months just like she promised.

But in a body bag.

There had been an accident on the set of her last film appearance. Apparently, the stagehands who dug and prepared the quicksand pit that day made it a little too deep. During the end of the shoot, when the two coked-up crewmen reached down into the goop to pull Ma Ruth out seconds after her Freddy Krueger face disappeared under the surface, they found themselves grabbing at nothing but quicksand. One of them had to dive in while the other held onto his legs. They eventually pulled the old woman out of the muck, but a little too late.

Ma Ruth was buried in a grave next to Tom Two and The Membrane. Per instructions outlined in her will, her cinder block gravestone was inscribed as thus:

HERE LIES

RUTH DOUGLIETTE LAMONT

BELOVED DAUGHTER, MOTHER, GREAT AUNT, GERIATRIC/QUICKSAND/FREDDY KRUEGER FETISH PORNSTAR

1928 – 2020

RIP

***

On a slightly more cheerful note, not long after Ma Ruth passed, Glont got hired to work for the Zeke Creek Coal Mining Company at a mine located about an hour southwest of Selohssa, allowing him to finally quit his hated "job" at Fun 4-Life.

Working as a coal miner was hard and the hours were often long. As such, Glont felt the job was a great improvement over working at Fun 4-Life. But there were problems. For one, the pay was great. Also, the mine had a nearly spotless worker safety record with no serious accidents having ever occurred. The company also offered a great benefits package—unmatched in the industry—and provided all employees with generous PTO and paid holidays so that workers could maintain a balanced work and family life. What's more, all the supervisors and managers at Zeke Creek were good-natured, concerned about the well-being of their employees, and highly receptive to feedback and criticism from even the company's lowest ranks.

To fully realize his long-time dream of working a shitty, miserable, go-nowhere, soul-crushing, hell-on-earth job, Glont sought to change these wonderful things. With that in mind, he joined the United Mine Workers of America union shortly after his hire and quickly rose in the ranks to become the representative union shop steward at the mine. Within a year of his appointment to shop steward, Glont succeeded in lowering all the miners' salaries by 20 percent and eliminated many of the successful safety measures that had been in place at the mine for decades, thereby causing a 13-percent increase in fatal mining accidents as well as a 23.7-percent increase in reported worker respiratory illnesses caused by overexposure to hazardous coal dust. He was also able to reduce the PTO and paid vacation time offered to employees to next to nothing while abolishing all available medical insurance, dental insurance, life insurance, and retirement plans. Glont also succeeded in getting all of the cool, good-natured, empathic supervisors and managers fired and replaced with blithering, insufferable, inconceivable, unbearable, cruel, sadistic, slave-driving fucking motherfuckers.

Within a year of getting hired, Glont managed to make his job terrible enough for him to finally be happy. By then, he was working fifteen-hour shifts without any days off for shit pay. What's more, he was fortunate enough to suffer from a plethora of coal dust-related lung diseases, among them pneumoconiosis, silicosis, dust-related diffuse fibrosis, and chronic obstructive pulmonary disease. And lucky for Glont, he didn't have health insurance anymore so that these conditions had to go completely untreated, thereby increasing his physical and mental misery. Glont was even lucky enough to be involved in a serious workplace accident when a mine shaft partially collapsed, killing nine of his coworkers while trapping him and twelve others for nearly two weeks. Glont suffered a crushed leg in the accident. Luckily for him, it had to be amputated after they pulled him out of the mine. The accident was the direct result of Glont greatly reducing the minimum structural support safety standards for newly drilled mine shafts!

Though he was down to one leg and had one heck of a cough, he got around the mine shafts just fine by pushing himself around in a mine cart. Fortunately, just after Ma-He's-Makin'-Eyes-At-Me discovered she was with child, the couple had to declare bankruptcy and foreclose on the Lamont ancestral home due to Glont's self-imposed abject poverty, but it was okay because he knew a place where they could live for free. Immediately after the foreclosure, he, Ma-He's-Makin'-Eyes-At-Me, and his invisible mother-in-law moved into the Selohssa sewer system, where they took up residence in Old Crub's old abandoned lair, a low igloo-like hovel situated at a juncture of four wide sewer tunnels. The thing had been constructed from a hodgepodge of junkyard scrap materials. Glont expanded it and even added on a nursery.

Sadly, Glont never got to see his baby. A week shy of Ma-He's-Makin'-Eyes-At-Me's due date, the blindfold that Glont wore to bed every night (for obvious safety reasons) came loose and slipped off his head while he was tossing and turning in his sleep. When he and his wife stirred awake the next morning, they opened their eyes at the same time while facing each other, their noses nearly touching. Neither of them was fully awake, so that they didn't think to turn away to save Glont's life. Husband and wife then stared into each other's eyes for the first and last time.

Glont was buried near Tom Two, The Membrane, and Ma Ruth. Due to her poverty, Ma-He's-Makin'-Eyes-At-Me couldn't even afford a cinder block grave marker for her husband, so she stole an old toilet from the local junkyard and used that instead. The inside of the toilet bowl was encrusted with petrified shit, vomit, and blood.

According to local Selohssa burial regulations, all cemetery grave markers had to display the legal name of the deceased at the time of their death. As Glont had never bothered to officially change his name back to Glont Lamont, his grave marker had to show his name as "My Tiny Little Weak Bitch." But with that exception, the exact words and characters specified in his will were inscribed on the underside of the raised toilet seat lid. It read thusly:

HERE LIES

MY TINY LITTLE WEAK BITCH

SON, FATHER, UNCLE, HUSBAND, COAL MINER

1979 – 2022

RIP RIP RIP RIP RIP RIP

FUCK FUCK FUCK FUCK

SHIT SHIT SHIT SHIT

FUCK FUCK FUCK FUCK

SHIT SHIT SHIT SHIT

FUCK FUCK FUCK FUCK

SHIT SHIT SHIT SHIT

THE END THE END THE END
THE END THE END THE END
THE END THE END THE END
THE END THE END THE END
THE END THE END THE END
THE END THE END THE END
THE END THE END THE END
THE END THE END THE END
THE END THE END THE END
THE END THE END THE END
THE END THE END THE END
THE END THE END THE END

ABOUT THE AUTHOR

Born with one extra finger and two extra toes (like, for real), Douglas Hackle received a B.A. in English Literature from John Carroll University, abandoned academia to take a writing-intensive job in the business world, and lost a few marbles somewhere along the way. He lives in Northeast Ohio with his wife, son, and two dogs. He is also the author of the novel *The Hottest Gay Man Ever Killed in a Shark Attack*; the Wonderland Award-nominated short story collections *Clown Tear Junkies* (Rooster Republic Press) and *Is Winona Ryder Still with the Dude from Soul Asylum? and Other LURID Tales of DOOM and TERROR!!!* A selection of his short fiction is featured in the *The Bizarro Starter Kit – Vol. Red* (Eraserhead Press).

douglashackle.wordpress.com

Made in the USA
Columbia, SC
25 March 2023